The Summer of My Fourteenth Year

By

Jim Meaders

Argus Enterprises International
North Carolina****New Jersey
www.a-argusbooks.com

The Summer of My Fourteenth Year
© 2009
All rights reserved by Jim Meaders

A-Argus Better Book Publishers, LLC

For information:
A-Argus Better Book Publishers, LLC
Post Office Box 914
Kernersville, North Carolina 27285
www.a-argusbooks.com

ISBN: 978-0-9841642-2-9
ISBN: 0-9841342-2-0

Book Cover designed by Dubya

Printed in the United States of America

DEDICATION

First off, this first leap into writing is dedicated to Dorian, my wife, for putting up with me all these years and for loving me and encouraging me.

Secondly, *The Summer of My Fourteenth Year* is dedicated to all the young men and women from my generation who died young, especially in Southeast Asia, and never got to grow old and remember the summer of their fourteenth year.

Chapter One

It was the Memorial Day weekend before the upcoming summer when I would turn 14. It didn't make much difference if it was Memorial Day or not. Dad had to work at his service station Saturday, Sunday, and Monday and mom was only off on Sunday when she would catch up on the laundry, ironing, sewing, and other household chores that dad and I either didn't or wouldn't do. Things were pretty much normal for a mid-Florida late May day: warm, dry, and I was thinking about my first car that I would buy, with dad's help of course, when I turned 16. The only problem was that I had to start mowing yards to save up the money to buy that first car.

1963 was nearly half gone and it had been the usual uneventful year so far that one experienced growing up in a small town almost anywhere, but it especially seemed to be that way for a relatively shy, moderately nerdy, soon-to-be ninth grader in this small Florida town of about 40,000 people. It was nearly 8:30 in the morning and I had just finished my Saturday chore of washing and drying the breakfast dishes. Dad had left at 6:00 that morning to get to his station and open by 6:30, and mom had caught the 7:30 bus to town to get to her job in the notions department at the five and dime by 8:00. I had wasted about 30 minutes watching cartoons on the television and could have easily wasted the whole day if I hadn't been thinking so much about my first car. That set me into motion on the breakfast dishes so I could get out and start earning some money mowing yards.

I got my Schwinn bicycle, a Christmas present three Christmases ago, and the lawn mower, the gas-powered, walk behind, push-type with a three-horsepower motor, out of the storage room at the end of the carport. I found a short piece of clothesline left over from the new clothesline that dad had put up for mom just last weekend in the backyard and tied the mower to the back of my bicycle. Now all I had to do was find where dad had put the gas can. I found it behind the wringer washing machine and secured it to the mower with another piece of clothesline. I found the hand grass clippers and put them in the carry bag hanging off the back of the bicycle seat and attached a broom to the mower as well. Most of the time people wanted their driveways trimmed, thus the hand grass clippers, and swept. I was now all set to peddle off down the street and start earning lots of money for that new car I was dreaming about.

All of the immediate neighbors mowed their own yards or, like my parents, made their kids do it as part of their chores. That meant biking at least two to three streets over to find people who might be willing to pay two to four dollars to have their yards mowed. Two dollars for yards around 1/4 to 1/3 of an acre and four dollars for up to an acre. It was a judgment call on my part when they asked how much I charged and sometimes I charged too little to mow too much. These prices for mowing yards were the going rates at the time for kids my age to charge, which were usually two to three dollars less than the "professional" yardmen who had pick-up trucks for hauling their larger mowers. With any luck at all I could mow five yards today and make at least ten dollars on my first day out.

I had ridden my bicycle up and down the surrounding streets as far as twenty to thirty blocks away, not that my parents ever knew that, but really hadn't noticed the houses and yards very much. I had to ride five streets over from mine before finding the first lawn that looked like it needed mowing. It was obviously a two dollar yard, but it didn't have a paved driveway and that meant a shorter time spent on the job. I pulled into the driveway, got off my bicycle, and walked up on the front porch. There was no doorbell so I knocked hard on the door, in case an older person lived there who couldn't hear too well. About a minute passed and I was getting ready to knock again when a woman who appeared to be in her sixties opened the door. She didn't say anything at first but only looked at me with that "Who the devil are you and what the devil do you want?" look on her face. Now kids in those days were taught, for the most part, to respect their elders and in some cases even fear them. This was one of those "fear" cases. The look she was giving me made me almost stutter and forget why I was there, but I mustered up my courage and asked if she would like to have her yard mowed.

"How much ya git fer mowin' a little ol' bitty yard like thisun?" she asked in a very pleasant voice, but still with that look on her face that would have frozen a grown man in his tracks.

"Two dollars, ma'am," I replied.

"I'll give ye one fifty and toss in a glass of milk and sum cookies," she politely responded.

"You wouldn't happen to have a RC Cola would you?" I questioned.

Her eyes got bigger, her head cocked to one side, she straightened up a little and in a slightly deeper voice said, "Smart little monkey, ain't cha?"

"No ma'am," I responded with a shaky voice and thought to myself, *This isn't the way things are supposed to go. She was supposed to simply say yes or no and we would go on from there.*

"Well, I ain't got no RC, but I do got some home-made rut (pronounced like put) beer ye kin have, but ye'll only get two cookies with that."

"That's fine, ma'am. I'll be through in no time."

"Jes knock when yeer thru and I'll have yer money and treats ready in the kitchen."

The deal struck, she closed the door and I got everything untied and cranked up my mower. About forty-five minutes later I had finished mowing the yard and hooked all my equipment back up to my bicycle. I knocked on the door and when the old woman opened the door she simply motioned me in and closed the door. She shuffled past me in worn out, pink bedroom slippers and motioned for me to follow her. We went to the kitchen at the back of the house where she had a glass with an amber colored liquid in it and two cookies on a simple white plate sitting on a small red kitchen table. There was only one chair at the table and she motioned for me to sit. I did as directed and reaching into her apron pocket she pulled out four quarters and five dimes and placed them on the table.

"Eat yer cookies and drink yer rut beer and when yeer finished take yer money and leave by the kitchen door," she instructed and then she shuffled out of the room. Just as she left the kitchen she turned around and stuck her head back in asking, "Can yer come agin in two weeks?"

"Yes ma'am, I'd be happy to," I responded.

"Then so be it," she said and shuffled off.

Hot doggy, I thought. *A regular gig. Maybe I can get some more of these.* I ate my two cookies, which were obviously homemade ginger bread cookies, and drank my homemade "rut" beer, which actually tasted just like regular bottled root beer, and left by the kitchen door one dollar and fifty cents richer.

My mom would be coming home on the 5:30 bus and dad would probably be home around 7:00 that evening if he didn't have a big job to get done before Sunday working on someone's car. That meant I had to be back home by 5:00 so I could get cleaned up and be ready to help mom with dinner. It was already after 10:00 that Saturday morning and I had only mowed one yard. I needed to "git my butt in gear," as Dad would tell me sometimes when I wasn't working fast enough to suit him.

I got back home about 5:10 after having only found three yards to mow that day for a grand total of six dollars and fifty cents. And neither of the last two suggested me coming back again. When I told my dad this he just shook his head and asked me why I hadn't suggested it instead.

"You still ain't learned to use your head for something besides a hat rack, have you, James?"

"No, sir, I reckon not." It hadn't even occurred to me that I could be THAT bold. However, I did ask for an RC instead of milk. *Maybe I was bolder that I thought, just not too smart when it came to business matters.*

"So, was the cookies and root beer worth fifty cents?" he asked.

"They were real good! Homemade even!" I exclaimed trying to justify the loss of income for a snack.

"A bottle of root beer cost ten cents at the station and your mother has plenty of homemade cookies here you can take with you next time. I'll even pay for the root beer for you and you can charge that ol' biddy the two bucks you deserve," he told me with that air of seriousness he got when he thought someone was trying to gyp us.

"Yes, sir," I said knowing that I wouldn't dare ask to change my "arrangement" with the "ol' biddy."

I would just have to find 25 pop bottles over the next two weeks to turn in at two cents each without my parents knowing about it to make up for that fifty-cent loss of income. That wouldn't be too hard since there were always lots of pop bottles scattered along the roadside. The thing that torqued me off, however, was that I would usually have spent that fifty cents in pop bottle refunds for cigarettes and candy for myself. Yeh, I had started sneaking cigarettes when I was about ten or eleven and then figured out a way to buy my own when I was twelve. Kids could buy cigarettes in those days because there weren't any laws against it and merchants either didn't care or believed you when you said your father had sent you to get his cigarettes. Of course, I had to keep them hidden and only smoke when my parents weren't around. Since my dad smoked about three packs a day, they were only twenty-five cents a pack, I always smelled like cigarette smoke anyway and could smoke in the house when my parents weren't home.

Well, tomorrow was Sunday and I would either have to stay home and help Mom around the house or go with Dad to his service station and pump gas, wash windshields, check tires and oil, and even occasionally wash someone's car for two dollars, which went in the till to help pay the bills. My plan, as usual, was to go with Dad. I actually enjoyed being around the service station and watching him work on cars. That and once in a great while some hot babe would pull into the station for gas with her skirt hiked way up so that washing the windshield wasn't so bad. That was also why some of my buddies hung out at the station sometimes and "helped out" for free. I remember one hot day when I was sixteen and working after school at the station that Dad had to go to the auto parts store on the other side of town. He hadn't been gone more than five minutes when one of those "hot babes" whipped her sports car into the station and up to the pumps. She appeared to be about college age and was driving a new Mustang convertible, and let me tell you, her skirt was really hiked up! Now I was nearly six feet tall at this time and looked older than I really was, and when I started washing her windshield she squirmed around in her seat so that I even caught a glimpse of her panties! If I hadn't been so dang shy I could probably have gotten further than just stuttering through collecting for the gas and telling her thank you. But, alas, that was not to be a day that I could brag to my buddies about.

Chapter Two

School was out and I had the opportunity to go out mowing almost every day. However, being the typical almost fourteen year old I didn't exactly take advantage of this opportunity every day. There were other important activities that an adolescent boy did during the summer besides trying to make money. There was riding my bicycle into unexplored neighborhoods, often with one or two of my buddies. There was girl watching, especially when I would take the bus downtown sometimes to meet up with my mom for lunch. What I did before and after lunch was my business. There was lazing around the house watching TV all day or listening to records. And there was that all-important activity of just wasting time, doing absolutely nothing! There was nothing worse, well almost nothing worse, than interrupting an adolescent boy doing nothing. That time was sacred. For example, there was the time when I was sitting on the step in the carport watching ants march back and forth across the concrete and wondering where they were going when the telephone rang. Now who would be bothering to call our house in the middle of a perfectly good summer afternoon meant for watching ants? Well, I knew that I had to answer it because "it might be important." And as I kind of suspected, it was my mother checking to see if I had done my chores and if so, why wasn't I out mowing yards to make money to buy that car I wanted when I turned 16?

"Well, you better not be loafing tomorrow or you'll never see that car!" my mother almost yelled at me through the receiver.

"Yes, Mother," I sorrowfully replied.

"Don't you yes me, young man. You PROMISE me you're going to get your lazy butt up and try to earn some money!" she did yell this time.

"I promise," I said as sincerely as I could manage, and I DID mean it.

My mother was only about five foot four, but she wielded a big stick, actually a switch off the closest tree, and wasn't afraid to use it.

Well, that all said, the next day I hooked up my equipment to my bike and off I went in search of my fortune mowing yards. And it actually turned out to be a pretty good day and I didn't have to pedal too far from home, only a few blocks. I got three yards on the first street I tried, two on the next, and one on the sixth for a total of fourteen dollars that day. I was so tired, however, by the time I finished the third yard that I couldn't even pedal by bike and had to walk it home dragging the mower behind.

The next morning started out ok until I realized that the hand grass clippers had "disappeared" during the night! Who would take them? Or worse, which one of my parents had hidden them to punish me for being "lazy?" I called them both at work and confronted them about it. That was a huge mistake! After being yelled at by both parents and having my little bit of dignity dragged through the mud, especially by my mother, I did as instructed and set out to find those clippers. They had better not come home from working hard all day and discover that I hadn't found those clippers I was told, OR ELSE! My adolescent mind couldn't even begin to imagine what "OR ELSE" would mean in this case. After all, that was a nearly new $1.99 pair of the finest hand grass clippers that S.H. Kress & Co. carried. I had a sneaking suspicion, though, that I would have to cough up two bucks of my hard earned money to replace them if I didn't find them.

I spent at least half the day retracing my steps and combing over the yards I had mowed the previous day looking for that nearly new $1.99 pair of hand grass clippers. Did I find them, you ask? How shall I put this politely? NO! But I know where they disappeared or I'm pretty sure where they disappeared or I would at least bet that the grouchy old goat at the fourth house I mowed knew where they were. He followed me around the whole time telling me my blade was too high here and too low there and I missed a spot over there and I was doing a pretty shoddy job for two dollars. Talk about one indignity after another. He paid up, but I'll bet he took my clippers to make up for the "shoddy job" I had done. I had no doubt in my mind that he had taken my clippers and that was what I would tell my parents when they got home and didn't find the clippers in the shed. All I had to do next was figure how and when I would get even with the old goat.

Well, I only got two yards mowed that day, but they were both three dollar yards and that wasn't too bad. The bad part came, as I suspected, when I had to give two dollars of it to my mom to get a new pair of clippers the next day at work. Did they believe my story? Sure. They were even familiar with "old man Swebter" and figured I had to be telling the truth, but that still didn't replace the clippers. However, I wouldn't have to cough up the two bucks if I wanted to go back to old man Swebter's and ask him to please give me the clippers back. *No way!* He would probably chop me up with my own clippers, barbecue me, and then eat me to get rid of the evidence! Well, he wouldn't do that my parents assured me, but they wouldn't insist on me going back if he frightened me that much.

Whew! That was a close one! But something happened that night at the supper table. Before that night my father would have made me go back and confront old man Swebter, even after dark!. He would have made me do it even if it meant him taking off work and dragging me up to old man Swebter's front door and waiting for me to confront him. At which time Dad would have discovered the terrible truth – THAT I HAD ACTUALLY LOST THE CLIPPERS. Now that piece of information would have brought a much more severe punishment than coughing up two bucks. That piece of information would have brought out the two-inch wide, extra thick solid leather "I'LL TEACH YOU TO LIE TO ME" brown belt that hung on the back of my parents' bedroom door, and which my father was very adept in using in a most persuasive way!

Here's the interesting thing that happened that night at the supper table: my parents, BOTH of my parents, had softened up just a little. They might not have realized that they did that and if they did they probably didn't think I was smart enough to see it. I watched them carefully. There weren't any funny little sideglances at each other when it happened, it just happened. Besides trying to figure out what I was going to do to old man Swebter, because I still believed that he did take my clippers, now I had to figure out what I had done to manipulate those two people who were playing the part of my parents. Why had that moment of softening happened? *What had I done or said or how did I say whatever it was that I said to make it happen?* This was going to take some serious "time wasting" to figure out. And that brought up another problem: how was I going to find time to waste when I had to be out mowing my butt off to earn money for that car I was dreaming about getting when I turned 16? *Whoa! Wait a minute! Now I've got FOUR problems: trying to find yards to mow, how to get even with old man Swebter, figuring out why my parents went soft on me, and when to find the time to think about the third problem. Dear God in Heaven, I was growing up! I was starting to have life problems to solve instead of just being me! But wait! Maybe that was why my parents went soft on me, because I was growing up. That had to be it! Eureka!* I had solved problem number three and four and it didn't even take much time to do it. Yep, I was becoming an adult for sure. How could the hot babes not see that?

Chapter Three

What kind of car was I going to buy with all the money I earned over the next two summers? My favorite car was a Corvette, but the few hundred dollars I might earn wouldn't even make a down payment on a Corvette, even an old one, and, besides, there wasn't any way my parents would let me get a car like that. I would probably end up with something safe like a Rambler. Woo, woo! That would attract hot babes about as fast as the nerdy guy in my math class last semester. Jules "20 pens" Cleveland Van Burisen, III, if you can believe that. Besides the twenty or so ink pens usually found in his flower-print shirt pocket, there were the extra thick glasses, the highly-polished, black dress shoes, the trousers that were two inches too short, the white jockey underwear that always showed when he bent over because he tucked his shirts inside his underwear, and the brown satchel that he carried ALL of his textbooks in ALL of the time. But I digress. Back to the problem of figuring out how not to get stuck with an old four-cylinder Rambler with four doors and an automatic on the column. I guess my second choice after the Corvette would be a '56 or '57 two-door Chevy with a screaming 327 cubic inch engine, four on the floor, dual exhaust, mag wheels, and a bench seat in the front. Surely you don't have to ask why a bench seat? To skip forward two years, it was even worse than I had imagined! Dad helped me buy a 1959 four door Studebaker Lark that had been owned by a "retired lady school teacher" and which boasted a whopping 169.6 cubic inch flat head six cylinder power plant that went from zero to sixty in the neighborhood of 21 seconds, which felt more like 21 minutes. It even had the original plastic seat covers still on the back seats and which good ol' Dad wouldn't let me remove. And as the salesman at the Northside

Used Car Lot told my dad, "It's a real cream puff and a great deal for $400.00." Dad haggled the price down to $250.00 and I dug out my hard earned cash and paid for the "cream puff." And worse than not even thinking about cruising for hot babes, I had to drive this thing to school where I got ridiculed more than Jules did back in junior high.

Back to dreaming about what my first car would be, not knowing that every car I thought about would end up being just that, a dream. There were the 1955 through 1960 T-Birds (I didn't care for the newer ones) or how about a 1957 Porsche 1600 Super Speedster or a 1958 Buick Special convertible or a 1959 Triumph TR3 or any hot looking babe magnet. I was sitting out on the doorstep again while this critical decision making was going on in my important doing nothing time when the telephone ringing brought me back to reality. It was no doubt my Mom checking up on me and if I answered the phone then she would know that I was wasting time again. Solution, don't answer the phone. I would just tell her later that I was out looking for yards to mow when she called around 10:00 that morning. And just how stupid is an almost fourteen year old boy whose mind is on cars and girls? So stupid that when she mentioned at supper she had thought about calling me that morning that I blurted out without thinking that I was out looking for yards to mow around 10:00.

"I didn't say I called at all," she said with that polite yet cold you're in deep do-do voice.

"You stupid ignorant moronic ding dong do-do headed piece of crap," I thought to myself.

"Did the phone ring around 10:00 this morning?" Mom asked without showing any anger in her voice, yet.

"Be cool and collect yourself," I thought before answering. "How should I know? I wasn't here. Don't you usually try calling around 10:00? And if you're asking that then you obviously didn't call."

Now that statement was almost as bright as saying I was out mowing yards around 10:00. Basically, I was calling her stupid! And it stung right down to the quick, because the look on her face didn't just say OUCH, it said HOW DARE YOU THINK I'M THAT DUMB!

"I know you're lying to me mister," she said about as calmly as she could without blowing her stack.

"Are you lying to your mother, son?" Dad asked.

"No sir," I meekly replied.

"James!" my mother almost yelled. "I know you're lying! Do you think you're too old to get a spanking?"

"No ma'am," I replied even more meekly than before.

"You better get off your sorry butt and get out of this house early every morning to find yards to mow if you have even a smidgen of an idea about having a car to drive to high school in a couple of years! Do you understand me?" She was definitely yelling now.

"Yes ma'am," I replied ever more meekly.

"What? I can't hear you," she said in a slightly lower tone.

"Answer your mother, son," Dad said, knowing not to get into this any deeper.

"Yes ma'am," I piped up a little louder still with the picture of my tiny little mother spanking me vivid in my head.

"You just better see to it, young man," mom replied in a cooler voice. "Now get these dishes done and there will be no TV tonight for you. And another thing. I'm going to ask Mrs. Kiches next door to watch and see when you leave every morning."

Mrs. Kiches was about the same age as my parents and didn't have to work because her husband worked for the city and made good money as I often heard her tell my mother. And worse than being watched by Mrs. Kiches was that her son, Kelvin, would no doubt hear about this right down to the threat of the spanking. Kelvin was in the same grade as me, though a year older, and would be sure to spread this tidy little bit of information around when school started back in the Fall as he was a big fat jerk off who liked to torture me in any way he could. Oh well, just one more grown up problem to worry about. Getting older sure was a big pain in the patooty!

Chapter Four

It was time to get back over to the old lady's house where I had the root beer and cookies and mow her yard again. I wasn't supposed to ask first, just mow the yard and then come to the door to get paid (and have rut beer and cookies, of course). I got an early start so that I could look for more yards to mow after I was finished at the "root beer lady's" house as I was now calling her. I finished mowing the yard and went up on the porch and knocked on the door to get paid as instructed the first time I was there. The "root beer lady" came to the door and invited me in and took me back to the kitchen for my treats and money. Today there were two chairs at the little table and I thought to myself that this might take longer than expected. She probably wanted to talk about her grandchildren or something along those lines and I would just have to be polite and suffer through it.

We sat down and the first thing I noticed was two one dollar bills lying on the table next to the plate of three cookies. I turned to look at her and she was simply smiling at me like we were old friends or something.

"I don't have any change," I offered, "but I can run home and get some."

"No need, yungin," she replied. "It's all yeern. From now on, yeer gonna git two dollar."

"Thank you, ma'am," I replied. "It sure is appreciated. I'm saving up to get a car when I turn sixteen."

"Ain't never had no use fer no autimobill. I's taken the bus when I's need to git someswhere," she stated matter of factly.

"My mom has to take the bus to work every day," I said. "She hasn't ever learned to drive and besides we only have one car and my dad needs it to get to his job at the service station."

By the way, yungin, what's yeer folks call youns?" she inquired.

"James," I said.

"That there's a mite gud name fer a boy yungin," she almost proclaimed. "James wuz one of the twelve apostels, bruder of John, and son of Zebedee, in the Bible, yee knowd."

"Yes ma'am," I agreed, both feeling proud and ignorant at the same time since I didn't have much knowledge about the Bible. I had been going to church even though my parents didn't go, but I had missed a few Sundays here and there and I wasn't much for Bible school.

"What's your name?" I asked.

"Well now, that there's a interesten question, Mr. James," she said with a suspicious sort of look in her eye, even almost frightening. "Ain't yee gonna et yeer cookies and drink sumtin?"

That was a sly way to get around answering my question, but I decided not to pursue the matter if she didn't want to tell me her name. I took a bite of one cookie, ginger bread again, and then a slurp of what I thought was going to be rut beer again. *Holy cow, I thought! This isn't root beer! Maybe she was trying to poison me!* Then I realized that it was RC!

"You got RC!" I exclaimed louder than usual and with a big smile.

"Yeer jist enjoy, Mr. James, and I'll be back shortly," she said as she got up to leave the room.

"Thanks," I said after her.

Well now, I thought, this old gal isn't going to be so bad after all. Hell, I'll even sit and chat for a while if she wants. I finished my cookies and slurped down my RC and waited for maybe five minutes before the old gal shuffled back into the kitchen carrying a black book. She shuffled over to me real close and handed me the book.

"This here's fer yeer to borry until youns is edji-cated," she said. "I's wantin yous to read a page a day as long as weuns knowd each udder."

I took the book and turned it over to the cover and realized it was a Bible.

"I have a good Bible at home," I said, handing the Bible back to her. "You don't have to give up yours for me."

"I's got dozens of Bibles, boy, an I's want yous to have thisin," she said in a rather demanding voice. "As a fact of the matter, yous jes keep thatun."

She practically shoved the book under my arm and said, "It's time fer yee to git goin now. Yous be back in two weeks now, ok?"

"Yes ma'am," I replied, and added, "I still don't know your name. What do you want me to call you?"

"Yous dun got that there figgered out now, dun't yee?" she said giving me a look that once again was somewhat frightening.

I looked at her with wide eyes and in as unknow-ing and questioning of a way that I could muster.

"Yous kin call me Mrs. Rut Beer Lady if yous like," she said in a very strange voice that she hadn't used before.

Chapter Five

I practically ran to my bicycle after I got out the back door and left her driveway in a cloud of dust; well, not really, but it certainly felt like I was going that fast! *How could she have known I had been calling her that in m*y mind? I hadn't told even my best friend that I was calling her that. And I certainly would not have told my parents, because they sincerely believed in respecting other folks, especially if they were older than you. This was really creepy and I knew that I wouldn't be able to stop thinking about it for the next two weeks, just before I had to go back and mow her yard again. *Was Mrs. Root Beer Lady some kind of witch? Or worse, was she the Devil in disguise?* I decided pretty quickly that she couldn't be a witch, *didn't they live in caves or something?* Certainly not in neighborhoods with normal people. *And the Devil wouldn't give someone a Bible, would he? Maybe she was one of those gypsy types that you see at the fairs and carnivals and circuses who read your palm and tell your fortune for a quarter.* I was certainly convinced at this point that she could read my mind. Now I was worried what I had been thinking about when I was in her house before. I couldn't remember. I was too scared and confused to remember. I just had to tell somebody about this. *Didn't I?* But who would believe me? Even my best friend would make fun of me in this case. And I couldn't tell my parents, because they would first get on to me about making up false stories about people and then get on to me for calling people names, even though I hadn't called her a name out loud.

That was the beginning of what would turn out to be one strange day. I must have pedaled as fast as I could with lawnmower in tow for five blocks before I remembered why I was towing a lawnmower in the first place. Slow down James, I thought to myself, you've got to find more yards to mow and you probably just passed a whole bunch. Trying to refocus and slow down I was passing right in front of a yard that definitely needed mowing. I came to a screeching halt and jumped off my bicycle to assess the situation. This yard was at least a half acre and really overgrown. *Did I want to even try to mow it with my dinky old three horsepower push mower? Well, the yard needs mowing and I needed the money and I might even get away with asking five dollars to mow this one.* I walked up the concrete sidewalk and up on the front stoop and rang the doorbell. I waited for about a minute and had turned around to leave when I heard the door open behind me. I turned around to see that the door was barely open, no more than six inches, and a soft woman's voice asked if she could help me. I explained that I was out looking for yards to mow when I saw that her grass was getting a little bit long. I asked her if she would like to have it mowed and she replied that that would be nice. She said it in a way that made me think she thought I was going to mow it for free. I needed to perfect my sales pitch some for those who might misunderstand.

"I'll have to charge you five dollars for a yard this size with grass this long," I ventured.

"That'll be just fine, sweety," she said in the sexiest voice I think I had ever heard. "You just go ahead and do what you have to and when you're done come on in the house and I'll pay you. Is that ok, honey?"

"Yes, ma'am," I said and leaned a little to the left to see if I could get a peek at who I was talking to. She had moved about halfway out from behind the door into the small opening and my eyes feasted on a knock-dead gorgeous blond woman who couldn't have been more than 30 and who was dang near naked! She was wearing only a skimpy bra and panties and I had never in my life ever seen such a vision of beauty!

"Now hurry along, sweety, and get the yard all purty for Monica, ya hear?" she literally cooed at me.

The door shut softly and I felt like I was staggering back out to my bicycle to get my mower. I usually got the mower untied in about ten seconds, but I was shaking so much that it felt like it took me ten minutes. I finally got the mower untied from my bicycle and cranked it up and started mowing this lovely creature's beautiful grass. *Whoa! Hold on here!* I don't talk all mushy like that! A guy catches a glimpse of a pretty woman, ok, knock-dead gorgeous blond, and he starts talking like a girl? If I said those words to any of my buddies they would laugh me out of town and all the way to Pluto! *Hey, Jimmy boy, pay attention to your mowing. You missed a whole strip back there. Get your mind on your business and off that knock-dead, nearly naked gorgeous blond in the house.* Yeh, well tell that to my "raging hormones" as I had heard adults say when talking about adolescent boys! I was going to have to look that one up, because I still wasn't sure what it meant even though I was nearly fourteen. And then I lost sight of what I was supposed to be doing again when I heard her voice in my mind say Monica. Could there be a more beautiful name in the universe? *Ok, Jimmy boy, snap out of it!* You've got a lot of yard with tough long grass to mow and the day isn't waiting on you, as my father would have said.

It took me nearly two hours, but I finished mowing the yard and trimming the sidewalk and hooked my mower back up to my bicycle. I went up on the stoop again and rang the doorbell so that I could collect my money (and hopefully get another peek at that vision of beauty) and leave more frustrated and confused than when I got there.

When Monica answered the door this time she was standing behind it and opened it wider and invited me in, saying, "I thought I told you to just come on in when you finished, little darlin."

Well, my heart was racing at about the speed of light and I knew the whole neighborhood could probably even hear it thumping in my skinny little chest. I took a couple of steps into the house and turned to face her as she gently closed the door. This time she had a long nightgown on, but it was somewhat transparent and I could still see the outline of her bra and panties. My buddies wouldn't believe this either so here was another little secret I was going to have to keep to myself. Besides, if they did believe me they would want to tag along next time, assuming there would be a next time. She told me to wait right there and she would go get my money from the bedroom. I was so nervous I couldn't have moved if I had wanted to anyway. I had never been around a woman that was so darn sexy! She came back into what I figured was the living room of her small, but very trim and tidy, house and stopped right in front of me, no more than six inches away. I was so excited and nervous and scared all at the same time that I couldn't budge from my spot. She was so close that I could smell her flowery perfume. *Dear God*, I thought to myself, *please don't let me faint and look like a total jerk off.*

"Here's ya money, honey," she almost proclaimed. "Can you come every week and mow my yard?" she asked me in that soft, sexy voice.

"You betcha!" I blurted out. "I can come anytime you want!"

As soon as those words had cleared my lips I realized what I had said and HOW I had said it and I know I must have turned redder than the stripes on the American flag!

"Well, I'll be looking forward to seeing you again next week then," she said, as if we were already the best of friends.

"Yes, ma'am," I said a little too enthusiastically, "and I'll certainly be looking forward to seeing you, too!"

Oh crap! I did it again. You stupid little screw up, I thought to myself while turning a little redder in the process.

"One other thing, honey," she said as I was trying my best to open the door and leave. "What's your name?"

"Ja-James," I stuttered.

"Well, Ja-James," she smilingly said imitating my stutter, "my name's Monica and that's what you'll call me. Understood?"

"Yes, ma'am, uh, Monica," I managed to get out without stuttering this time. "If I mow your yard every week, . . . Monica, I shouldn't charge you so much because the grass won't be as long."

"Well, that's awfully sweet of you, James, but I'm glad to pay five dollars for such a good job," she cooed. "If I don't pay you five dollars then I'll have to make it up some other way," she said teasingly while winking at the same time and closing the door before I could embarrass myself again.

As I stood there on her stoop I realized that I must have looked awfully childish to such a beautiful, sophisticated lady. *There you go again, Jimmy boy, with that mushy talk.* I must have stood there for at least a minute when I realized that I was sweating up a storm. I was just a big bundle of excited, nervous, scared, embarrassed, raging hormones that would have both nightmares about Mrs. Root Beer Lady and wet dreams about Monica all the next week. Once again I thought that it must be really hard trying to grow up and I wasn't so sure that I was as excited about that as I had once been.

Chapter Six

The rest of that day was fairly uneventful except for finding four more yards to mow. I barely got home in time to help my mom with dinner. I lied when asked if anything exciting had happened that day, just mowed six yards including the old woman's a few blocks away. I didn't find all the rest until later in the afternoon I lied again and that was why I was running late getting home. Mom asked me if there were going to be any repeat jobs from the other five yards and I lied once again telling her I didn't think so, at least no one said to come back again. No way I could tell her about Monica, because I was afraid my parents might just check out the yards I was mowing more than once. I just couldn't get that lovely vision out of my mind. I had to tell someone about Monica. I didn't want to tell my buddies, even my best friend, more because I was afraid they would believe and want to tag along next time to get their own peek. No way that was going to happen! Monica was all mine! I thought about telling my girlfriend, Leasure (yes, that was her name), but then she would probably get all jealous and break up with me. Yes, at thirteen and in the eighth grade I had a girlfriend. Actually, it was more like I knew a girl who was a good friend. Her parents would bring her by for a visit once in a while, but only if my parents were home. And about half of the time she drug along her less than pleasant friend Lanelle so there was never any alone time with Leasure. However, if I had known at that time that Leasure was going to find that she was too good for me once we finished the ninth grade and went on to the tenth grade and high school then I would have told her the whole torrid story.

Well, I didn't tell anyone about Monica, but I did ride my bicycle past her house everyday (twice a day most of the time) as I went out looking for more yards to mow. Strange thing was that I never saw her or any sign that anyone even lived there except when I went back a week later to mow her yard again. Being the sly kid that I thought I was I sauntered up on to her front stoop and rang the doorbell with adult authority, whatever the heck that was. A few seconds passed and then the door opened about three inches and I heard her beautiful, soft voice tell me to go ahead and mow the yard and she would see me after I finished and the door closed. As hard as I tried I didn't see a dang thing that time. What a waste of a perfectly good saunter, one that I had been practicing all week. I even slipped up and sauntered when some of my buddies were around. They just laughed at me and wanted to know why I was walking so stupidly. Well, just who was the "stupid" one now? After all, I was the one mowing Monica's yard.

So I set to work wondering why she was hiding from me. *Could it be that she wasn't quite ready to let me see her this time?* That, of course, had to be the reason. She was undoubtedly putting on her sweetest perfume and skimpiest negligee just for me so that I could see her in all her wonderful loveliness. *There you go again, Jimmy boy, talking like a girl. If your buddies could hear you now you wouldn't have any buddies any more. They would stomp your butt and call you all kind of names set aside for "guys" like "that." And they would never let you live it down. So quit sauntering and talking like a girl and start acting like a man! That's what your father would tell you, as he often did when you started whining about anything. If you went back to her door walking and sounding like a "girly boy," Monica wouldn't let you step one foot in her house again and would probably tell you never to come back. BE A MAN, SON, as good old dad would say!*

When I had finished mowing the yard and trimming the sidewalk I practically ran back to Monica's front door anticipating seeing her in the skimpiest possible negligee ever designed by the greatest skimpy negligee designers in the world and smelling like a rose garden. I rang the bell and when the door opened I nearly screamed and fainted and felt like running like a scared dog! Standing before me wasn't that vision of beauty that I had seen the week before, but old Mrs. Root Beer Lady! *What the devil was going on? Where was my Monica? What had the old witch done with MY Monica?* I was too shocked and dumbfounded to know what to do next! I just stood there gaping at old Mrs. Root Beer Lady, my eyes wide and my mouth open. *I must be hallucinating! That's it, I mowed over some funny mushrooms and breathed the air and now I was hallucinating. That HAD to be it!*

"Well, quit yer starin youngin and take yer money. A doller fifty ain't it?" she asked. "I ain't got no RC or cookies today so youens jes run on along now and Is'll see ya next time. OK, Ja-James," she cooed.

I was speechless to say the least, so I grabbed the money and ran as hard as I could to get to my bicycle and get out of that place.

"Ain't ye even gonna say thankee?" she hollered behind me.

"Thanks," I yelled back without turning around to see what kind of horrible apparition was standing in the doorway now.

Had to be a dream, had to be a dream, wake up Jimmy boy, wake up Jimmy boy. But my bicycle just kept rolling along down the street as fast as my skinny little legs could pedal. *How had I ended up at the old lady's house mowing her yard instead of at Monica's house?* I slammed on my brakes and came to a skidding halt that almost dumped me over the handlebars of my bicycle. I looked at a nearby street sign and this WAS the right street. The old lady lived blocks away. I didn't know what was happening and right then and there I didn't want to know what was going on. I had to think about this for a while before coming to any hasty decisions. All I could imagine at that moment was that the old lady really was a witch and that she had killed Monica and eaten her. The old witch was probably doing that all over the surrounding neighborhoods. *How am I going to stop her or even tell others to be wary of her? No one, I MEAN ABSOLUTELY NO ONE, is going to believe this either. Thank God none of my buddies had come along today to see that vision of beauty.*

Chapter Seven

That very unusual and harrowing day was a Friday as I remember because I kept thinking that I could think about what had happened over the weekend. I asked my parents at the breakfast table on Saturday morning if I could stay home that day, because I was awfully tired from mowing so many yards on Friday. To my surprise they agreed. It was a surprise because up until that day they had been riding my case about getting out and finding more yards to mow. I was never going to earn enough to buy a car if I didn't and they definitely were not going to go in debt for another car just so I could go hotrodding around the city. But they agreed that I could stay home and rest that Saturday. I couldn't believe they were going soft on me again, probably some kind of psychological trick to show me that missing one day of mowing would eventually cost me that car I was dreaming about. But I figured I would play along and stay home anyway. I would make it up the next week.

I had it all figured out for that Saturday. My plan was to do a little snooping around both Mrs. Root Beer Lady's house and Monica's house to try and figure out what was really going on. Of course, there was the possibility that I would find nothing but blood everywhere in Monica's house because the old witch had killed and eaten her. And what if I got too close to the old witch's house and she caught me? My parents would never know what had happened to me. I thought about leaving a note as to my plans so that the police would be able to figure out how I had disappeared, but what if nothing happened and someone found my note before I could get rid of it? That would certainly be a hard one to explain.

I knew the surrounding neighborhoods well enough by now to be able to go sneaking around without it actually looking like I was sneaking around if anybody saw me. I had decided against leaving the note because things were either going to turn out to be normal or that I really had been hallucinating the day before. Surely I had just gotten turned around and confused on Friday and ended up mowing the old lady's yard by mistake and she was kind enough to pay me anyway. That had to be it.

I left the house around 8:15 that morning thinking that most of the adults had to go to work and no one would notice the "yard boy" sneaking around the Root Beer Lady's house or Monica's house. That was, of course, except for nosey old Mrs. Kiches who would tell my mother later that I had not been at home all day. When my mother heard this from Mrs. Kiches she asked her if she had been peeking out her window all day? Of course not she told Mom, And my mother, sticking up for me for once, asked her if my bicycle had been gone that day, because I didn't go anywhere without my bicycle. The bicycle, of course, was there every time she looked, but that didn't mean I was home. Well, Mom had had a bad day at work and she lit into Mrs. Kiches with a full arsenal of swear words the like of which Dad and I later agreed we had never heard before! Especially coming from Mom. Mom told Mrs. Kiches that she was one sick old b*%#@ who needed to mind her own d%*# business and keep her fat a** nose out of our business and try tending to her own screwed (she actually used the "f" word) up little b#*@%#$ w*#@% boy! Well, Mrs. Kiches was flabbergasted and just turned with tears in her eyes and stomped away. All Mom said when she came into the house was that she had better not find out that I had been lying to her.

Getting back to my mission, I took all the back yards and alleys that I knew to sneak first over to Mrs. Root Beer Lady's house. I had sneaked along the fence of the house behind hers and had settled at the corner to see if I could detect any motion in her house. The surrounding houses appeared to be quiet so I figured no one would notice me and even if they did they wouldn't say anything. Just some neighbor kid playing hide-n-seek. I must have squatted there for thirty minutes watching carefully all the windows I could see from the back side of her house and especially watching her backdoor. After squatting for that long I painfully stood up and let my legs wake up and get back to normal. When the tingling had finally stopped I decided to make a break for the cover of her back porch. I looked around and didn't see anyone and then ran as fast as I could for her porch. Her back porch was raised off the ground about three feet and supported by cement blocks at each corner so I quickly scooted under the porch to wait in hiding. The back porch was just off the kitchen where she seemed to spend a lot of her time so I tried to be as quiet as possible and not breathe any harder than I had to. I stretched out in the dirt under the porch and listened intently for at least the next thirty minutes, but I didn't hear even one little shuffle coming from inside the house.

I decided that the old witch must not be home and that I should probably sneak on over to Monica's house and check out the situation there. The old witch was probably over there anyway cleaning up the bloody mess she had made when she killed Monica and ate her. Maybe Mrs. Root Beer Lady needed to eat younger women so that she wouldn't keep getting older herself or she was some sort of creepy alien from outer space who had come down to earth to feast on humans or she was a cannibal from some far off land who had moved here because the "food" supply in her country was dwindling because her kind had eaten almost everyone there! The vivid imagination of a nearly fourteen year old boy could come up with some rather strange ideas sometimes.

I arrived at the house that I believed to be Monica's and carefully sneaked up on it "private eye" style all bent over and looking around constantly to see if anyone was watching me. I didn't see anyone watching me, but then when I was here yesterday I thought I had mowed Monica's yard and instead the old witch Mrs. Root Beer Lady came to the door to pay me. I was now leaning flat up against the back of Monica's house, "private eye" style, and still glancing back and forth to see if anyone was watching me. Then, to my horror, I looked into the backyard of the house behind Monica's and there stood an old man watching me.

"Whatcha doin over there sonny?" he inquired.

Trying to think fast I replied in my best scared silly squeaky lying voice, "I just came by to see when she wanted me to mow the yard again."

"Oh, yer the yard boy, ain'tcha?" he casually acknowledged.

"Ye-Yes, sir," I tried to say without stammering, but that didn't work either.

"Well, why ya been mowin that there yard fer anyway?" he asked. "Ain't nobody lived there for five or six years."

Now that was a revelation I both didn't want to hear or need to hear. This old coot had to be crazier than a loon!

"But a lady has paid me twice for mowing the yard," I said thinking that two ladies had actually paid me, hadn't they?

"Aw, yer crazier than a loon!" he exclaimed. "How can ye git paid if'n no one lives there? It's nice of ye to mow the yard and make it all purty, but ain't no one payin ya cause no one lives there."

"Yes, sir." I conceded and began to walk away toward the front of the house where I would ring the doorbell and just see for myself when one of the women would answer the door and I could prove I was right.

I turned to look back once as I neared the front of the house and the old coot was still watching me. I went around to the front and up on the stoop and rang the doorbell, except that it didn't ring. Ok, that's weird I thought, because I KNOW that I had heard the doorbell twice before. Maybe I was crazier than a loon like the old coot at the house behind had said and maybe I even imagined him! I jumped off the end of the stoop and ran back around to the backyard to see if the old man was still out in his yard. Well, at least I wasn't totally crazy. There was a house behind this one, but the old man wasn't anywhere in sight. There was a chain link fence around his backyard so I went around to the front and up on the porch where I rang HIS doorbell. A few seconds passed and the door opened. A woman I guessed to be about forty, my mom's age, stood behind the screen door and asked me if she could help me with something. Thinking fast again I said I just wanted to apologize to the old man I had been talking to in the backyard just a few minutes ago. I told her that I thought he might have misunderstood me and I didn't want him to think badly of me.

"What kind of sick joke is this and just who are you?" she said with a quiver in her voice. "My father has been dead for nearly six years you impudent little brat! All of you brats are just sick, sick, sick!" she practically yelled at me and slammed the door shut.

Well, I slinked down her sidewalk and back to my house feeling lower than a snake's belly and slimier than slug goo. *No doubt about it!* I was either crazier than a loon or had one heck of an imagination! At this point I was almost hoping it was the former rather than the latter. Oh how I hoped that Mrs. Kiches hadn't seen me slip out that morning, because with all this craziness swarming around in my head I couldn't even begin to think up a good enough lie to cover my butt that day.

Chapter Eight

When I got back home on that Saturday, I just crashed on the sofa until my mom got home from work. I was too tired and certainly too confused to do anything productive. I was sound asleep when my mom came in the door. I didn't even wake up when the door closed and she had to shake me awake. She wanted to know how long I had been asleep and I told her it must have been several hours. I guess I just needed the rest I told her and she agreed. Now on any other day that in itself would have been strange, her agreeing with me so readily. But after what I had been through, or thought I had been through, the past couple of days her agreeing with me didn't seem out of the ordinary at all.

Besides Mrs. Kiches getting chewed out by Mom a little later after Dad got home from work, the rest of the evening went pretty smoothly. After dinner and helping with the dishes I crashed back on the sofa in front of the TV. Dad was watching one of his favorite sitcoms, *The Beverly Hillbillies*, and I made it about half-way through before falling sound asleep again. My parents didn't bother me until they got ready to go to bed around 10:00 and then woke me up and sent me off to my room. I was sure that I would have nightmares that night, but I once again fell into a deep sleep and didn't stir until Mom yelled in at me to get up and get ready for breakfast. It had been raining during the night and was still raining that morning at breakfast. Dad said it would be a slow day at the service station and why didn't I stay home and help my mother around the house.

That was fine with me and I helped around the house by sweeping, dusting, and cleaning up my room. About mid-morning I was finished and mom put me to work straightening up the shed at the end of the carport. It was around lunchtime when that was finished and mom fixed us each a fried bologna sandwich and we sat quietly at the dinner table eating. I was amazed at how little she had to say that morning.

She observed that I still looked awfully tired and said I could watch TV that afternoon if I wanted. She was even going to take it a little easy before having to fix dinner. That sounded good to me and once again I crashed on the sofa and went right to sleep.

I did dream this time and it did have to do with recent events in my life. My dream started out nice, however, but didn't stay that way for very long. I was reclining on Monica's plush divan with my head resting in her lap and her fingers running through my hair. After what seemed like a mere few seconds of this she suddenly turned into the gross old witch of Mrs. Root Beer Lady except that this time the old hag had long sharp fingernails and fish-like scales all over her gnarled and wrinkled naked body. YUK!! The old woman had grown to twice her normal height and had lifted me by my hair and was dangling me up in the air like a ragged old doll. Then she made this awful screeching sound and the old man who lived, or had lived, behind Monica's house appeared in the kitchen doorway except that he was much fatter, naked, and had the same reptilian skin that the old woman was sporting. His mouth opened at least three feet wide and a flickering green tongue issued from his mouth and began licking at my feet, which I noticed were now bare. Then he went down on all fours and crawled closer and the old hag dangled me over his gaping mouth and began to lower me into what now looked liked a huge hole in the floor with jagged teeth completely surrounding it. I was yelling for her not to feed me to the old man when I was shaken awake by my mom.

At first I thought my mom was the old hag who was trying to feed me to the big fat man-lizard thing and I pushed frantically back into the cushions of the sofa. She shook me again and told me I was having a nightmare and that everything was ok. It took me a few seconds to calm down, but I was still shaking as the last images of my dream were still running through my head.

"What in the world were you dreaming about?" she asked with just a hint of fear in her voice. "You scared me nearly to death."

"There was this horrible old woman who was trying to feed me to a giant lizard," I told her in a still nervous voice.

"Well, where in the world would that kind of idea come from?" she asked.

"I don't know. Maybe it was something I ate," I ventured.

"Well, you've done enough sleeping for now. Maybe you should go outside for awhile," she suggested.

"Ok," I said and went out to get some fresh air.

As my luck would have it, Kelvin was also outside on their carport, which was next to ours with only about ten feet of yard separating the two carports. He was tossing a tennis ball against the wall and catching it when it bounced back. As soon as the door shut behind me Kelvin called to me to come over to his carport. I knew this wasn't going to be good, but I didn't want to look like a wussie either so I ventured into his territory.

"Listen you little weenie," he said in his best angry voice. "First time I catch you alone when there ain't no adults around I'm going to pound your puny little butt in the ground all the way to China!" he literally snarled at me.

"What did I do to you?" I asked as calmly as I could realizing that even though I could easily outrun him, I didn't have many places to run.

"It's what your crazy old lady said to my mother that's going to get your skinny little butt whipped," he said with determination.

"I'm not responsible for what she says," I offered as a kind of excuse.

"Don't matter cause you're the one's going to suffer!" he practically shouted. "Now get off our property."

His mother yelled from inside, "Kelvin, what are you yelling about out there? Try to keep it down will you!"

"Yes, Mother," the fat bugger politely replied.

I just couldn't help myself, especially since I was back in our yard and close to the door from the carport to the kitchen, so I taunted back with, "Now who's the weenie?"

Kelvin made like he was going to lunge for me, but I had the kitchen door open and was headed inside faster than he could say "weenie" and with the middle finger of my left hand waving bye to him just before the door closed behind me.

Well, I was very careful the rest of that summer and made sure that Kelvin and I weren't ever alone without there being adults within shouting range. The rest of my plan to avoid Mr. Kelvin Kiches was to collect as many adult eastern lubber grasshoppers as possible. I had no fear of these large yellow and black grasshoppers that seemed to always be everywhere in Florida. However, I found out early on that Kelvin was scared to death of them and let me tell you I thoroughly enjoyed either tossing them at him or fending him off and chasing him with one clasped between my skinny little fingers. I collected ten or twelve over the next few days and kept them in a shoe box with holes punched in it in the shed, feeding them grass and flower petals on a regular basis. *Come near me Kelvin "Mommy's Boy" Kiches and I'll have a big old lubber spitting all over you before I toss him in your hair!*

Chapter Nine

Monday morning rolled around and I had to get the mower back out and start looking for more yards to mow, only this time I was heading in the opposite direction that I had been going. New territory to both explore and look for yards to mow. I didn't have to venture back into the old territory for a few days, maybe even next week, to mow the two or three "regular" customers' yards, and I wasn't going anywhere near Monica's house and I was very reluctant to go back to Mrs. Root Beer Lady's house, especially after my nightmare. I just knew that my dream was some kind of warning to stay away from those houses and that area in general. The only problem I foresaw at the time was if my parents asked me if I had mowed the old lady's yard recently. Well, I had lied before, I guess I could lie again. Lying seemed to get easier each time you did it, but there was always the consequences of lying to one's parents looming in the back of my mind if they found out. And there wouldn't be any way to logically explain why I had lied either.

I cruised up and down three streets before I came to one that looked like it needed mowing. I parked my bicycle on the sidewalk and walked up the gravel path to the stoop and front door. This was an oddly colored house in that it was bright green with pink shutters and a red door. *Oh well*, I thought, *each to his own.* There wasn't a doorbell so I knocked hard and waited a few seconds before the door opened. I nearly pooped in my pants when the door opened wide and there stood the old man I had talked to on Saturday, the one who had been dead for nearly six years! My mouth was hanging open, but no words were coming out.

"Well, looky who's here," the old guy blurted out with an uneasy air of enthusiasm. "You come by to mow my yard?" he asked very politely.

"I-i-i-if you wa-wa-want me to," I managed to stammer through.

"Why, there isn't much that I can think of that I would like better than to have you mow my yard," he said looking at me in a strange sort of way, but with a big grin on his face. "Would five dollars be fair," he asked me matter of factly.

"Ye-ye-yes, sir," I responded unable to quit stammering. All I could think of was what he looked like in my dream and what he was going to do to me.

"Well, you better get at it then, because I'm sure you have more yards to mow today," he said, sounding a little bit like my father. As a matter of fact, he sounded almost exactly like my father.

I hurried back down the gravel path and got my mower cranked up and started mowing his yard. The grass wasn't too long, but it might be in a few days. People who walked by probably thought I had lost my mind or invented a new way to mow yards, because I mowed in a circle around his house so that my back was never toward the house. I wanted to be able to see the old hag if she burst from the house to get me so that I could get a head start running from her. I figured I could out run her to my bicycle and escape before she could grab me. Of course, I wasn't taking into consideration my lawn mower or that if she came out the back door the old man could come out the front door and cut me off before I could get to my bicycle. If that had occurred to me I would have probably jumped on my bike and pedaled on down the street and not mowed the yard in the first place. But you have to remember that I was a nearly fourteen-year-old inexperienced, naïve young lad whose imagination was running wild, so I couldn't think of everything!

Besides mowing in a circle around the house so that I could keep an eye on all the doors and windows,

I also started next to the house so that with each circle of the house I would be farther and farther away from it, thus giving me a little more of an edge in the distance that would be between me and the old hag if she burst from the house to get me. I thought that that bit of strategy was downright genius. Well, nothing happened to me while I was mowing the old man's yard and that gave me plenty of time to think about how he could be here in this house when I had seen him at the other house and when he was supposed to be dead. I just needed to get control of myself and start thinking more logically, at least that is what my dad would have told me in addition to saying I was too old to be conjuring up imaginary friends. *FRIENDS? HA! What kind of friends play such terrible tricks on you and try to kill you and eat you? What was the old saying I had heard my mom use? "Friends in need are friends indeed." Well, in this case that should read "Friends who are hungry want to eat you!"* Ok, so it doesn't rhyme, but I didn't try to be a poet until my hippie years.

I finished mowing the yard and got my mower tied up real good to my bicycle before I went up to get paid. I was thanking God all the time that the old hag hadn't come after me so that I would have left the mower behind. Try explaining that one to my dad! I knocked on the door and moved back a few steps so that the old man couldn't grab me and pull me into his house where, no doubt, the old hag was waiting for her next human meal. The door opened and the old man stepped out onto the stoop and I moved another step back. He looked at me kind of funny, but then I probably looked like the most scared kid he had ever seen unless, of course, he and the old hag really were eating human children for lunch.

"I'm going to give you a ten dollar bill, sonny," he said, "because I won't be here when you come to mow the next time. That means you need to mow again in about two weeks. OK?"

"Yes, sir," I tried to say with reassurance, but it was much squeakier than my regular voice.

"Ok, then," he said. "Then when we get back shortly after that the yard better be mowed or I'll come talk to your parents about it."

"Yes, sir!" I assured him this time. "It'll be done just like you said."

I had taken the ten dollar bill from him and backed up a few more steps during this exchange almost falling off the stoop. Catching my balance I turned and jumped down the two feet or so and finished our conversation as I walked rapidly toward my bicycle.

"Don't you forget now or I'll have to come talk to your parents," he yelled after me as I rode away on my bicycle.

I didn't respond, but just kept pedaling as fast as I could to get away from there because I wasn't convinced that they still wouldn't come after me. As I was riding away from the old man's house his use of the word 'we' just sank in all of a sudden and I nearly lost control of my bicycle. *Holy cow! The old hag must have been in there with him! Why hadn't they tried to capture me this time? What was up with that? Maybe they really weren't going away for two weeks and they would be there waiting for me when I returned to mow the yard again. Maybe they liked their human children aged a little longer before they ate them. That made sense. You had to be closer to fourteen before you tasted just right to these reptilian aliens who could make themselves look like humans.* Maybe some of dad's SkeeterSkoot mosquito repellent that we slathered on when we went finishing at the old mined out phosphate pits would do the job for keeping reptilian aliens away from me. I could buy some at the neighborhood Rexall drug store where dad always bought his; actually, the only place where you could buy it since it carried the Rexall name. Mr. Gruds, the druggist, would think I was just getting some for when dad and I went fishing. It was cheap enough and I had a few extra bucks in my pocket so I could buy two bottles and really slather up before I went back to mow the old man's yard.

I actually got five yards mowed that day and was on my way back home. I had almost forgotten about mowing the old man's yard that morning when a car horn blared out and startled me. I turned to see if it was someone I knew and started to wave as a long black Cadillac cruised by slowly. Monica was driving and waving at me and peeking over from the passenger side and waving was the old man. *Was Monica the other half of the 'we' he had mentioned that morning? Surely not! How could she be involved with that old geezer? Not my Monica!* As the Cadillac came up even to me Monica blew me a kiss and I thought I would melt on the spot! I glanced at the old man and he was laughing hardily the whole time and then, as they went on past, Monica started laughing, too. Now what I'm about to tell you is going to make you think, maybe even KNOW, that I had to be delusional, but I swear it's the truth and I KNOW what I saw! As the Caddy slipped away from where I stood the trunk lid opened up about three feet and there was old Mrs. Root Beer Lady sitting in the trunk waving a hanky at me! I was so dumbfounded that all I could do was wave back. She started cackling, gave me the finger and shut the trunk lid down with a bang! I wasn't far from home and I began running as hard as I could pushing my bicycle and dragging the mower behind. I cut through several yards and down one alley to put them off my trail with the mower bouncing and bumping along behind the bicycle. It's a wonder that it didn't fall to pieces the way it rattled across the uneven ground. I came up to our house from the back side pushing my bicycle and mower around to the carport where I dropped the bicycle and fumbled for what seemed like minutes to get my house key out and get the door unlocked. I got the kitchen door open and literally jumped inside when I heard a car coming down the street. I slammed the door behind me and locked it and ran to the living room to peek out the front curtains. I just knew that the car I had heard was going to be the long black Caddy with Monica and the old man in it, having followed me home to see where I lived so they could come back after dark and get me! As it turned out it was only the neighbor across the street, Mrs. Maleway and her grandson Roger.

Chapter Ten

Roger was just about my best buddy, but even he wouldn't have believed any of my adventures of late. He lived with his grandmother because his mom and dad were divorced. His dad lived halfway across the country in Iowa and his mom had a small apartment somewhere on the other side of town. Roger told me he couldn't live with his mom because she didn't have the room and, besides, she had a lot of gentlemen calling on her at night. I overheard my mom tell Dad one night when she didn't know I was nearby that Roger's mom was nothing more than a redheaded harlot! I heard Mom say many times that it was a good thing Roger had his grandmother to bring him up right. Well, I guess what Mom and Granny Maleway didn't know wouldn't hurt them, as the old saying goes. You see, Roger had just gotten back from spending a week with his dad in Iowa and just happened to find in his dad's bedroom a collection of girlie magazines. Roger had managed to sneak one into his luggage before leaving his dad's place and being the trusting parent and grandparent that they were, neither Mr. Warstet or Granny Maleway even thought about checking Roger's luggage. Roger, of course, knew this and only hid the magazine inside one leg of a pair of pants. Tucking the bottom half down his pants and hiding the top half under his tee shirt, Roger couldn't wait to find me and show me his prize.

Now in those days girlie magazines usually only showed some breasts and not much more, but to two nearly fourteen-year-old boys with raging hormones that was more than they ever got to see in real life. It didn't take too long before the pages in that magazine were starting to come loose from the daily use it got by two best buddies. We were worse than two school girls giggling over passed notes in class as we passed the magazine back and forth, back and forth, back and forth practically drooling over the pictures of the well-endowed ladies posing on the pages.

Since Roger had been trusting enough to share his good fortune with his best buddy, I had decided to go ahead and tell him about my adventures of late. At first he looked at me like I was crazy, but then began to fall under the spell of the story and wanted to tag along the next time I went to mow any of the yards of the crazies, as he began calling them. I figured that was just fine with me since it would be harder for the old man and the old hag to catch two of us. If they did catch one the other could run for help. Roger was really anxious to meet Monica, especially since we had recently been educating ourselves in the physical attributes of the fairer sex. But I warned him that we should still be very careful around Monica, because I was pretty much convinced that she and the old hag were one and the same. I figured she first changed from the reptilian alien thing into Monica to lure young boys and then without warning became the scaly old hag of a thing that feasted on human flesh!

No matter, Roger wanted to see her and even meet her so he could get up close like I had. Well, it was getting close to the time when I should be mowing those yards again so I told Roger we would go out the next day to the three houses where these strange events had been happening to me. Besides, if Roger saw all these things happen then I could be pretty sure that I really wasn't mad after all.

Chapter Eleven

The next morning after my parents had left for work I went across the street to get Roger. He was ready to go and said he hadn't gotten much sleep thinking about Monica. We went back to my house to make a plan of attack for the day. We agreed to start at the old man's house hoping that he really wasn't back home yet and because I had already collected the money for mowing his yard. There didn't seem to be anyone home at the old man's house and so I started mowing as fast as I could. I had just finished and sat down on the front stoop with Roger to rest a few minutes when we heard a car speeding down the street. We looked up just in time to see the black Cadillac whip into the driveway and come to a screeching halt. Roger and I looked at each other wide-eyed and then back at the Caddy, both of us too scared to run. We both stood up at the same time and were just about to flee the scene when the driver's side door opened and out stepped Monica. Well, when nothing else could have stopped us in our tracks then the sight of that gorgeous vision of womanhood slinking around the front of the Caddy did the trick. Standing next to each other, eyes wide open, mouths gaping, and about to wet our pants Roger and I couldn't speak, blink, or move. Monica strode toward us wearing the skimpiest mini-skirt I've ever seen (even to this day), a halter top just as skimpy, and heels that had to be at least six inches high. I glanced sideways at Roger to see if he was still breathing only to see drool oozing from the side of his mouth. This Monica must have been at least six feet tall (the old Monica couldn't have been over five foot six inches tall), because when she stopped about twelve inches in front of us our eyes were level. I glanced again at Roger and knew that nothing intelligible was going to come from his mouth, just drool, and managed to stammer out a hello.

"Well, hello yourself you sexy young thang, you," she said in her best southern drawl. I was so mesmerized by all the gorgeous, sexy, exposed skin that I hadn't even noticed that when she spoke Roger had fainted dead away. When I got a smidgen of my senses back I poked my elbow at Roger to get him to speak. When my elbow didn't encounter anything I glanced first to my side then down behind me where Roger still lay unconscious with drool being the only thing coming from his mouth.

"H-h-hi ma'am I stuttered," realizing at the very moment I said it that I had already said hello to her.

"Looks like your little friend has a touch of heat stroke or something. Don't you think you should try to wake him up?" she seemed to innocently ask.

"Uh, yes'm," I responded in the stupidest voice I had ever heard myself utter. Whereupon I immediately went down on my knees next to Roger and started shaking him. "Roger, Roger, wake up dude before you miss everything!" I practically yelled at him.

As Roger slowly opened his eyes he raised himself up on one elbow and glanced past me and fainted again. I quickly looked back just in time to see Monica bending over to pick up something on the ground – bending over away from us. Poor Roger had only briefly glimpsed what I was now taking in with eyes as wide as I could make them, Monica's bikini panties that that showed off most of her gorgeous round butt cheeks. I stared for what seemed like several minutes, but was only a brief few seconds (however, that was a few seconds longer than Roger!), when Monica stood up and turned around to catch me with my head lowered and to one side.

"Why, you naughty little boy. You been looking up Monica's skirt. Haven't you?" she said in short but very deliberate little spurts.

I was still so mesmerized by this vision of beauty that the only thing I could think of to say was, "Yes ma'am. I cannot tell a lie. That's what I was doing." You can call me George or you can call me Washington, but I just couldn't lie to this beautiful "apple tree."

"Well, that's aw right," she said, "'cause boys will be boys."

"Yes'm," I blurted out with what sounded like pleasure in my voice. She really didn't mind that I had had me a peek.

"Ya'll certainly have something to tell your little friend when he wakes up," she said and then winked at me slyly. "Now, I'm going to pay ya'll twenty dollars if ya'll keep this our little secret. Is that ok with you, honey," she cooed.

Ok? Secret? Twenty dollars! "You betcha!" I nearly shouted as she handed me the twenty-dollar bill. I heard Roger stirring behind me and I quickly shoved the twenty in my pants pocket so he wouldn't see it. At that precise moment I glanced back at Monica and she just smiled knowingly at me and winked. The twenty would no doubt be our little secret.

Monica squatted down next to Roger as he was waking up and of course he fainted again because he was eye-level with Monica's knees and peeked straight up her skirt. Monica stood and walked toward the old man's house saying that she was going to get a cold wash cloth to put on "my little friend's head." What seemed like an eternity passed before she returned and I saw what had taken her so long. She was now wearing blue jeans and a loose fitting shirt. When Roger came around this time he didn't faint, but he did remain speechless. Monica informed us that she would now be living in this house and that the "old man," as she too referred to him, wouldn't ever be back again. She also told me, because Roger was still in a daze and didn't seem to be registering anything, that she was going to water the yard a lot and that she wanted me to come alone and mow every week and she would pay me ten dollars every time, but I had to keep our little secret. I wasn't exactly sure what she meant by "our little secret," but I was certainly going to keep it. If I played this right at home (and since Roger hadn't really heard any of this) I could mow fewer yards and still have the money as if I had mowed more. *What a gig this was going to be!*

Chapter Twelve

After about ten minutes Rogers finally came to his senses, or at least was able to walk around looking half alive. We tied the mower up to my bicycle and started off down the street to head to our next destination, which was going to be Monica's house. However, we really didn't see any sense in going there if Monica was now living in the former home of the old man, but that logic didn't stop us from following our curiosity straight to where I thought Monica lived in the first place. We were pedaling down Monica's former street like two vagabonds looking for their next place to crash when I brought my bicycle to a grinding halt in front of a vacant lot. Roger nearly wrecked his bicycle trying to stop after he realized that I had stopped.

"What are you doing, dummy?" he asked. "Let's get to that house and see what's going on there."

"I hate to tell you this old buddy," I replied, "but this is where Monica's house used to be."

Roger turned around, looked at the recently mowed vacant lot, and exclaimed, "You're banana crackers, dude! I think the heat's getting to you now!"

"No, man, this is the place!" Reaching in my left front pants pocket I withdrew a piece of note paper with all the addresses of the yards I had mowed written on it and told Roger, "I've got the address written on this piece of paper. Look for yourself. It's the number between that house and that house," pointing to both the mailbox behind us and the next one ahead of us.

Roger took the piece of paper, looked at it and then at me and then at the other two mailboxes and quietly said, "Does anyone else know that you are mentally deranged?"

"Ok," I ventured wondering if Roger was going to take the bait I was getting ready to throw his way, "you just go on home like the little fainting fairy that you are, but I'm going to find out what's going on around here and I'm going to do it now!"

"Ok, I'm sorry," he said in his most sincere voice, "but this mess is pretty spooky business if you ask me."

"No crap!" I exclaimed. "It's all starting to drive me crazy and no comments from the peanut gallery! Now let's go next door and find out what we can about this place, this vacant lot."

We pushed our bicycles slowly back to the house that we had just passed and up the driveway. We parked them facing back toward the street so we could make a faster get away, just in case this was another one of those weird houses where strange people, or reptilian aliens, lived. Roger didn't want to go up on the porch with me at first, but I grabbed him by the arm and literally slung him ahead of me and then pushed him toward the front door. He stood to one side while I rang the doorbell. A kindly-looking man about the age of my father opened the door and asked what he could do for us. I explained that I thought I had been mowing the yard next door, but there wasn't a house there now. He told us that we must have gotten the wrong street because that lot belonged to him and there had never been a house on it. He then kind of squinted at me and put on the glasses that he had hanging around his neck on a black cord.

"Well, if it ain't the little whippersnapper that mowed my lot this morning!" he said somewhat astonished. "If you think I'm going to pay you for mowing it you got another think coming! You did that job for free, sonny boy."

I looked over at Roger and he was staring at me with his mouth hanging open and then he started moving toward the steps up to the porch. I was carefully backing in that direction myself and said to the man in the door, "That's ok, mister, I needed the practice and I really wasn't here to try and collect for mowing it and we won't bother you anymore and so we'll be going now if that's ok."

"Kids today sure are strange," he mumbled as he closed the door.

Roger and I had an unplanned race to see who could get on his bicycle and get down the driveway first because we just knew the old hag, the Root Beer lady, was getting ready to spring out and grab us for lunch. Pedaling as hard as we could and gasping for breath we first agreed to head home for a while to figure things out (or hide).

At that moment I came to another screeching halt and Roger went zooming past for about a hundred feet before he stopped and looked back. He stared at me for a few seconds and then blurted out, "Oh no, no way, ain't gonna happen, dude!" knowing that I had already decided to go back and pursue this matter at the house on the other side of the vacant lot.

"Come on, man," I pleaded not wanting to do this alone. "You don't want us to be big fat wussies like Kelvin, do you?"

Well, that did the trick because nobody wanted to be a big fat wussie like Kelvin, especially Roger who got picked on by the big fat bully as much as I did. Without saying a word Roger got his bicycle turned around and started back toward me. He pedaled past me with that "you're gonna pay" look and I turned around and followed him back up the street to the other house. As a side note, Roger and I gave each other that look all the time. Roger was smaller than me and about a year younger and he knew that I could whip his butt. That "you're gonna pay" look was just what the best of buddies did sometimes. It kind of kept us on an even ground.

We got to the other house, parked our bicycles in the get-away position, and approached the front door together. I rang the bell and we waited for about a minute before a sweet-looking little old lady who must have been 110 opened the door. I'm sure her smile would have melted any grandchild's heart, but since I had never really known any of my grandparents it didn't have much effect on me. Roger, on the other hand, seemed to melt under the spell of that pleasant face smiling at him and with a big grin of peace and serenity on his face said, "Good morning, ma'am. We seem to be lost. We thought the vacant lot next door was a yard that we had mowed before and were supposed to mow this week, but we're obviously wrong because there ain't no house there. Has there ever been a house there?"

"Well, aren't you two just the little gentlemen," she said at first. "The man that lives on the other side of the lot owns it and won't sell it to anyone because he says he likes his privacy. Why, I've tried to buy it two or three times over the past forty years or so, but he just won't sell. I even offered him $700.00 for it a couple of years ago, which is twice what it's worth according to my daughter who's a real estate agent, and he wouldn't budge. Would you nice young fellows like to come in for some milk and cookies? An old lady gets awfully lonely, especially since her husband passed away ten years ago yesterday and her only child, that sorry daughter I was telling you about, hardly ever comes to visit." She stopped and smiled congenially at us looking from one to the other and back again.

Roger was just about to accept her offer when I took a step forward and said that we needed to get going and find that yard that we were supposed to mow. I had noticed how she had said "young" fellows and I didn't like it. Roger was well under her grandmotherly spell and had missed it all together. Of course, he didn't have as much experience with all these crazies as I did. I grabbed Roger by the arm and pulled him along with me back toward our bicycles.

"Oh, by the way," the little old grandmotherly look-ing woman yelled behind us, did the old grouch pay you for mowing his lot this morning?"

That was it! We jumped on our bicycles simulta-neously and shot out of her yard and up the street like racecar drivers at Daytona never even looking at each other, much less looking back at her. We both seemed to sense that if we looked back we would be turned into pillars of salt, just like in the Bible, or she would be chasing us down the street on her broom! Roger didn't even have to suggest that we go back home this time because I had already decided that I was going back and not coming out again all day for anything or any-body. Not even if Monica came to the door naked and begged me to take her then and there! Roger might have been as scared as me but I was about a half block ahead of him, with lawn mower in tow, when I got back to my house. Roger went straight to his house without even looking my way or saying any-thing. I knew that tomorrow we would sit down and waste the whole day contemplating these events. It's what best buddies did when they were perplexed about something – like girls, for example. Besides, even though "tomorrow was another day," we didn't want another day like this one. I wasn't even sure at that point if I would mow any more yards that summer. What about my car when I turned sixteen? As long as I scrounged up as much as I could I was pretty sure good ol' Dad would come through with the rest. I knew that somewhere under that rough exterior there was an old softy. Yep, tomorrow was another day.

Chapter Thirteen

I spent the rest of the afternoon raiding the fridge and crashing on the sofa. I didn't want to look out the curtains for fear that one of the reptilian aliens would be standing at the window waiting to jump through the window and eat me. Now you have to understand that this was 1963 and I was a nearly-fourteen-year-old boy with a fairly good imagination, but not with the best of logical minds of the time. Maybe that's why I grew up to be an artist instead of a mathematician. Of course, there was the five and a half years I spent selling shoes at the local downtown department store, but selling shoes didn't take logic, just an ability to BS the customer and make them believe that what you were selling was exactly what they wanted. Again, I digress. After stuffing my face with two large dill pickles, a big bowl of Neapolitan ice cream, a large bowl of Mom's homemade from scratch banana pudding, six slices of Sunbeam white bread (I especially liked the end pieces), a couple of tomatoes, and a raw sweet potato I decided to watch television. There wasn't a lot to watch in 1963, especially with the cheap antennae that Dad had attached to the side of the house and which extended about ten feet up past the peak of the roof. I knew that we couldn't afford a better antennae, like the Kiches had, but we only got three stations on our Philco television and the Kiches got five stations on their Sylvania television, as Kelvin often pointed out to me when we were watching his set on those rare occasions that I could stand to be around him. Nevertheless, I got up off the sofa, walked over to the set at one end of the living room, turned it on and waited for it to warm up, and then tuned into the new soap opera, General Hospital, on ABC. For some strange reason I just liked Dr. Steve Hardy and nurse Jessie Brewer and even thought I might like to be a doctor some day. Crashing back on the sofa I watched mindlessly until I dozed off. I dreamed that I was floating in a swimming pool of banana pudding casually scooping up a handful once in a while and stuffing it into my mouth. Little Miss Sunbeam was standing at the edge of the pool and trying to seduce me to get out by holding an end piece of bread from an open bag of Sunbeam Bread she held hanging down by her side. She winked at me and then took a tiny little bite out of the end piece of bread and held it back out at arm length shifting her weight to one foot in a more tempting pose (called contrapposto I would later learn at art school). But alas, this was Mom's homemade-from-scratch banana pudding and I had a whole swimming pool full of it and even Monica couldn't get me to come out of the pool! But then Little Miss Sunbeam turned to the life guard, a giant dill pickle shaped like a shark, and told him to rescue me. Well, the shark-shaped giant dill pickle jumped into the pool of banana pudding and started swimming toward me. I was ready to fight him off if necessary to protect my pool of banana pudding, but as he got closer he opened his mouth wide to expose his large, green, sharp teeth. At that moment I realized that I was going to be his lunch and that rescue wasn't in his vocabulary! Little Miss Sunbeam was now laughing so hard that she dropped the bag of Sunbeam Bread and fell off the edge of the pool head first into the banana pudding! Just as the shark-shaped giant dill pickle was getting ready to clamp down on me I jerked awake almost violently and fell off the sofa nearly hitting my head on the coffee table.

The television was still going, but General Hospital wasn't on now and according to the clock on the end table next to Mom's rocker it was almost time for her to be home. Not feeling too steady just yet I crawled over to the television and turned it off. I sat on the floor for a few minutes going back over my dream and thinking that maybe I should be more careful about what I snacked on after having a scary experience while out mowing yards. Maybe I would just stick to some banana pudding next time.

About that time Mom opened the kitchen door and came in to find me still sitting on the floor. I explained that I had been watching television and had fallen asleep and just woke up a few minutes before she got home from work.

"Another rough day out mowing yards?" she asked.

"Not too bad I said, but I didn't get much mowing done. Can I tell you about something that happened today?" I asked.

"You can always talk to me," she said matter-of-factly.

"Promise you won't make fun or tell Dad?" I sort of pleaded.

"Don't worry about that," she said. It was what she always said in these cases.

I proceeded to tell her about the day's adventures that Roger and I had experienced. I told her about going to this one house to mow the yard where I was supposed to have a regular gig and that there wasn't a house there and when I asked the neighbors next to the empty lot about it they said there had never been a house there. And the really strange thing was that they both said that I had mowed that empty lot that morning.

In her ever calm, logical way mom said, "Well, dear, the two old people just mistook you for some other young boy out mowing yards and you know how you and Roger horse around all the time. You just went to the wrong street."

"Yeh, that must have been what happened," I agreed, knowing full well that I wasn't that crazy. I know what happened, because Roger and I were both there and he saw and heard everything, too. However, there was one flaw in that: Roger would never admit to anyone what happened, especially not to an adult. "It was so hot out today that maybe the sun got to me," I offered.

"Well, you need to be careful about working too hard outside when it's this hot. Promise me that you will drink lots of water and rest once in a while in this heat," mom said.

"I promise," I responded. "I do drink lots and lots of water from people's water hoses when I'm mowing," I offered. There was nothing more refreshing than drinking from a garden hose on a hot day. I even held the hose over my head most of the time soaking my hair and face.

"That's good," mom agreed. "You do that all the time and you'll be just fine. Now, help me get dinner started so it'll be ready when your father gets home. How about setting the table for me and then peel some potatoes for mashed potatoes. I'll get the water boiling."

Dinner went smoothly that evening without any mention of my day's activities. Dad seemed awfully tired that night and fell asleep soon after sitting down in his easy chair after dinner. Mom went all out that night because she knew that Dad had had a hard day at the service station rebuilding a motor in a 1959 Dodge Coronet. We had fried chicken, green beans cooked with some bacon grease, mashed potatoes and gravy, fresh homemade biscuits, and, of course, banana pudding for dessert. And, yes, I had another large bowl of banana pudding and no nightmares that night.

Chapter Fourteen

The next morning rolled around and everything seemed to be just fine. After my parents left for work I moseyed over to Roger's grandmother's house and knocked on the door. I was hoping that Roger would go with me that day in search of more yards to mow, but when Granny Maleway came to the door she informed me that Roger had come down with something, probably a summer cold she thought, and she was going to keep him inside all day. As I turned to walk away somewhat disappointed that I was going to have to go out alone that day Granny Maleway wished me luck in finding some yards to mow.

Now I figured Roger was still scared from the day before and was faking being sick to get out of going with me. I'd confront him about it later and threaten to tell his granny about the girlie magazine if he ever copped out on me again. Roger wasn't much of a thinker, but more of the kind of person who would just go along with the crowd, especially if it seemed safe. He was also pretty easy to intimidate when it came down to the nitty-gritty of a situation. Usually, if I ignored him for a day or two he would come crawling back around and want to get back in the action. It was either hang out with me or get hassled by Kelvin.

I had already decided to venture into some new territory today, which meant crossing the busy four-lane boulevard that I wasn't supposed to cross. My parents rules said: "You will NEVER ride your bicycle across Memorial Boulevard. Is that clear?" It was perfectly clear and I knew the consequences of doing so if they ever found out that I had ridden my bicycle across Memorial Boulevard. However, being the creative individual that I was I had already come up with a plan that would work because it meant that I would not have to go across memorial Boulevard. What my parents hadn't thought about and probably didn't think I was smart enough to think about was that I could go down to the railroad yard and walk my bicycle along the tracks under the Memorial Boulevard overpass that went over the railroad tracks and which would take me to the other side of Memorial Boulevard without riding my bicycle across it.

Emerging on the other side of Memorial Boulevard I was feeling pretty good for myself for having outsmarted my parents. I was just coming up to the street that I was going to go down looking for new yards to mow when I looked up just in time to recognize the Kiches' 1960 ugly green AMC Rambler Custom Station Wagon coming around the curve. Fortunately for me there was an alley running behind some of the houses and I just happened to be even with it. I jerked my bicycle with mower in tow quickly down the alley and started running as fast as I could. I glanced back to catch a brief glimpse of Mrs. Kiches and Kelvin zipping past, but I would swear on a stack of the Root Beer Lady's Bibles that mine and Kelvin's eyes met ever so briefly and that his eyes got bigger in recognition of me. How could one kid be so cottonpickin' unlucky in everything I thought to myself sympathetically. If Kelvin saw me he would tell his mother, who never doubted what little Kelvin said when it came to me, and then she would tell my mother. The only plus I could think of in this case would be that my mother would cuss her out again for believing her lying son who was always trying to come up with stories to get me in trouble. Besides, I was forbidden to cross over Memorial Boulevard and if she asked me later if I had crossed over Memorial Boulevard I could honestly say no.

I kept going down the alley for a little ways before venturing out toward the street because I figured Kelvin would convince his mother that he had seen me and she might just circle back to find out for herself.

When I got out to the street I looked up and down it and didn't see any signs of the ugly green Rambler Station Wagon and so I proceeded on my way to find some yards to mow. I had never been in this part of town except when I was in the car when my dad was driving through. I wouldn't even have considered coming into this neighborhood except that I was trying to get as far away as I could from anyplace connected to the old man and Mrs. Root Beer Lady, and yes, even Monica. I would mow ten yards for free to get another look at her panties, but I still wasn't convinced that she and the old hag weren't one and the same. I had read somewhere that witches could change their appearance with just the snap of their fingers.

I hadn't gone very far when I came to a yard that definitely needed mowing and so I went up to the front door and knocked. A man opened the screen door looking like he just got out of bed and hadn't shaved in about a week. He also smelled of beer (my dad had the occasional beer so I recognized the smell).

"Whacha wont, kid?" he asked me, at which point I knew he had been drinking a lot and was definitely drunk. I'd seen my uncle drunk a few times and that was how he talked and smelled.

"I'm trying to earn some money this summer," I said, "and was wondering if you would like for me to mow your yard for two dollars?"

"Whacha goin ta spend yer money on, kid?" he tried to say more clearly, but it didn't work. "Gonna go ta town and buy ya a horse?," and he started giggling like a girl.

"No sir," I said trying not to both laugh and throw-up from the smell at the same time. "I'm saving up to get me a car when I turn sixteen," I announced proudly.

"Thas gud, cause a car's a gud place to get ya whur yer goin, if ya know whut I mean," he managed to get out just before he fell backwards onto his fat backside with a loud thump.

"Are you ok, sir?" I asked still trying not to laugh. Now I know being drunk isn't funny, but I was a nearly-fourteen-year-old boy who thought lots of things that weren't supposed to be funny were funny and this just happened to be one of those times.

"Yer a pulite little turd. Ya know dat?" He reached into his pants pocket and pulled out a wad of one dollar bills which spilled all over the floor next to him. Picking up two of the crumpled up ones he tossed them at me saying, "Cheers yer money. Now mow it gud soins the nosey nebors'll quit complaining. Kay?"

"Yes sir," I replied picking up the two dollars and heading back to get my mower untied from my bicycle. I had only gone a few steps when I heard another thump behind me and turning around I saw that he had passed out where he sat with the screen door still standing open for all to see. I went back and closed the screen door thinking that was the least I could do. I got the yard mowed in no time, tied my mower up to my bicycle and headed off down the street without going back to check on the drunk. Hopefully no one would come in and rob him while he was passed out.

Thinking that made me come to a stop and turn around and head back to the drunk's house. I went back to the front door and he was still passed out. I opened the screen door and pulled his front door shut and closed the screen door back. That should at least make people think that the house was locked up. I got back on my bicycle and headed back down the street to look for more yards to mow hoping that I wouldn't run into any more drunks.

The rest of the day went along just fine and I ended up mowing six yards taking in fourteen dollars. The rest of my customers for the day all seemed like perfectly normal people and I didn't suspect anyone of being a witch or the old hag or old man in disguise. My only real problems on the day were nearly being seen by Kelvin and his old lady (at least I hoped I hadn't been seen by them) and when I finished mowing the last yard realizing that it was late and my mom would be home from work before I could get back, especially if I returned the way I came. I could probably get back just a few minutes before her if I took the "high road" and went across Memorial Boulevard. It was a chance I would have to take and a lie I would have to tell later if asked about crossing Memorial Boulevard. I pedaled as fast as my skinny little legs would go and when I got to Memorial Boulevard the intersection was amazingly clear and I just zipped right across without even letting up pedaling. Mom was due home in 20 minutes and it was going to take me a good 15 minutes to get there.

I came around the corner and onto my street and still I hadn't slowed up. I came to a screeching halt in the carport not bothering to even untie the mower and put it and my bicycle away. Mom's bus wasn't due to run for another six minutes so I was in pretty good shape. I got my keys out to unlock the kitchen door, but to my horror it wasn't locked. I froze in my shoes right there on the doorstep not knowing if I should turn and run because the old hag had broken into my house looking for me or if I should go in and face whatever music awaited me. I slowly opened the door and peeked around the corner to see what might be awaiting me. I didn't immediately see anyone or anything so I cautiously stepped inside the house, closed the door behind me (which wasn't too bright if someone or something was waiting to jump out and eat me), and looked around the vacant kitchen and living room.

Then from out of one the two bedrooms at the other end of the house came a familiar voice, "James, is that you?"

I came about as close as I ever have in my entire life to wetting my pants right then and there! The voice belonged to my mom, or someone posing as my mom since she still hadn't come out of the bedroom in which she was hiding.

"Mom?" I cautiously asked.

"I'm in the bedroom, James," she replied. "I wasn't feeling well and came home early. I'm in bed."

I walked down the hall to my parents' bedroom and cautiously peeked in to see my mother huddled up under the covers shivering.

"I've got a fever, son," she told me, "so don't get too close."

That was some relief because I figured if it was one of the reptilian aliens disguising itself as my mother that it would want me to get closer, like the wolf in Little Red Riding Hood.

"You are going to have to fix your father's dinner tonight, because I just can't do it. Ok?"

"Sure, Mom," I replied, "but it will have to be pretty simple. "Can I get you anything right now?"

"No. Just put something together for your father. He'll be awfully tired when he gets home and probably pretty hungry."

"Ok," I said and turned to go back to the kitchen. She must have been really sick not to ask me why I was so late getting home or how many yards I had mowed. Just as I got back into the kitchen the door swung open and my mom stepped in and this time I not only pissed myself, but I screamed!

Chapter Fifteen

The scream shocked my mom, or whoever this person happened to be, as much as seeing my mom walk through the door had shocked me. She had dropped her purse and about half of the contents had fallen out. She quickly stooped down and scooped up the contents of her purse and when she stood back up she looked at me with eyes I didn't remember ever seeing before.

Then from behind me came my mom's voice saying rather loudly, "What in God's name is wrong with you, James?"

I turned around quickly to see my mom coming from the bedroom with her housecoat wrapped around her and still shivering, even though we didn't have an air conditioner and it must have been 90 degrees outside. I quickly swung back around to compare my two moms only to see no one standing there and the door standing wide open.

I turned back around and my mom (I was pretty sure this was my real mom now) was still standing there shivering and waiting for an answer to her question. "I've had a very tiring day mowing yards I said and when I came back out to the kitchen the door was standing open and I thought I saw a strange man peeking in," I lied.

"Well, close the door and lock it this time and get busy fixing your father something for dinner. When he gets home he can look around outside and see if he can find any evidence of someone prowling around. Now hop to it before I take a switch to you."

"Yes, ma'am," I said and closed and locked the door without looking outside. If the old hag was waiting just outside the door she could grab me and fly off on her broom before my ailing mom could take two steps.

"There's some leftover chicken 'n dumplings in the fridge and some cold cornbread on the stove from this morning," Mom offered. "Put the chicken 'n dumplings in a pot and heat it up slowly on the stove," she instructed me. "Put a little water in the pot so it doesn't stick. It should be warm by the time your father gets home. He won't mind that the cornbread is cold. There's a pitcher of ice tea in the fridge, too, and you can get him a glass of that to drink. Remember that he doesn't like ice in it. Ok?"

"Thanks, Mom," I said, and proceeded to get the chicken 'n dumplings out of the fridge. I was pretty hungry, too, and was hoping there was enough chicken 'n dumplings left for me to have some as well. Mom's chicken 'n dumplings were made from scratch and she often made me knead the dough because her hands ached all the time, probably from handling piece goods at the local five and dime all day. I also usually had to cut the strips and drop them in the boiling water to cook. I'm not sure what she put in the flour mixture, but she said there was a secret ingredient that her mother taught her to use and if I was good she would tell me what it was someday. My mom died in 1992 and I never did remember to ask what that secret ingredient was, but the chicken 'n dumplings at Cracker Barrel restaurants comes pretty darn close to tasting as good as I remember my mom's being.

Well, Mom went back to bed and Dad got home around the usual time looking like he had been "through the wringer" as my mom would often describe him when he got home. I explained to Dad that Mom wasn't feeling well and I hoped he liked left over chicken 'n dumplings and cold cornbread because that was what I had fixed. He said that was fine as long as they were what my mom had made. Dad loved my mom's cooking almost as much as I did, maybe even more. While we were eating our leftover dinner I told Dad what had happened with the door standing open and a strange man peeking in. He hadn't seen anyone hanging around the house when he drove in the driveway, but he would go outside and look around after dinner. He reminded me to always make sure the door was closed and locked behind me when I came home because you never knew what kind of a weirdo might be following me around. It was why we moved to this little town in Florida from Birmingham he told me. Birmingham had gotten too big and had too much crime to bring a kid up right.

I thanked him for that, but at the same time wondered if Birmingham had any old hags who were really witches and old men who turned into reptilian alien things that wanted to eat you. If Birmingham was ten times bigger than this town then there must have been ten times more old hags and reptilian aliens roaming around there. Of course, the up side would have been that there were also probably ten times more Monicas roaming around there. The big city must be an adolescent boy's paradise as long as he didn't get eaten up by aliens and witches.

It was almost dusk when Dad and I finished dinner. I cleaned up the table and started washing the dishes while Dad went outside to look for clues of a prowler having been around our house. When he came back in he said he didn't see anything unusual except my bicycle and mower still sitting in the carport in the way of him being able to pull the car all the way in. I had finished washing the few dinner dishes and said I would go put them away, but wanted him to watch from the door while I did so. He said that he had put everything away for me, but next time I would have to go outside in the dark by myself to put things away. Well, I guarantee you that after the experience of that afternoon I never ever again left my bicycle or mower or anything else out past dark. Dad and I were both really tired and went to bed early that night giving up watching any television. Even though I was really tired it took me a while to get to sleep because I kept thinking about the episode that afternoon with seeing two moms in the same house. The old hag had undoubtedly followed me home and thought she could grab me without my sick mom waking up or knowing why I never got home. I reasoned that if I hadn't been in such a hurry to get home before my mom did the old hag would probably have caught up to me and that would have been the end of little Jimmy boy! Fortunately, my dreams were peaceful that night.

Chapter Sixteen

A couple of weeks went by and nothing unusual happened when I was out mowing yards and I didn't see anyone prowling around our house during that time. Roger came around a couple of days after the "two moms" incident and, as it turns out, he really had been sick. His granny even had to take him to the doctor the next day after my adventure on the other side of Memorial Boulevard. I had gone off in another direction that my parents said was ok for me to go to look for yards to mow and I hadn't even given any thought to going back across Memorial Boulevard. I figured that if Kelvin had seen me that day that he hadn't said anything to his mom or I would have heard about it by now. Dad told me when I turned sixteen that Kelvin had told his mother about seeing me on the other side of Memorial Boulevard and that Mrs. Kiches had gone to my mom's work place the very next day and told her about Kelvin seeing me across Memorial Boulevard. Dad said that mom knew better and told Mrs. Kiches in no uncertain words and tone that I was forbidden to cross over that road and wouldn't disobey her. He said that mom had yelled at Mrs. Kiches again, this time in front of two of her best customers, and that the other ladies also lit into Mrs. Kiches sticking up for me. I hadn't seen Kelvin during that two weeks. It was highly unusual for the big bully not to follow up on this little episode with all kinds of threats. As it turned out, for whatever reason, Kelvin had been sent to his grandmother's farm in Georgia for a few weeks.

My birthday was just three days away on Sunday, July 21, and I was no longer going to be an almost fourteen year old boy, I was going to be a F-O-U-R-T-E-E-N year old boy. Dang near a MAN! And best of all, that much closer to getting my first car! Dad had promised that he would take me down on Monday to get my learner's permit and that he would start teaching me to drive on weekends. By the time I turned sixteen and had to take Driver's Ed in high school I had been driving for two years. Most of the kids in my class had never even been behind the steering wheel of a go-cart, much less a real car.

The summer of 1963 was obviously important to me, if not VERY strange. But it was one of those years when a lot of bad things happened and a lot of important people died, and thousands of young American men were preparing to die in Vietnam Nam. Pope John XXIII died, as well as W.E.B. Du Bois, Robert Frost, Aldous Huxley, and of course John F. Kennedy was assassinated. But, on the brighter side, quasars were discovered, the first commercial nuclear reactor went on line, Valium was developed, The Beatles were starting to "take Britain by storm," the Rolling Stones emerged as the "anti-Beatles," Julia Child debuted on educational television (not that we could get educational television), the Dodgers took the Yankees in the World Series in four, Boston defeated the Lakers in the NBA Championship, Chateaugay was the Kentucky Derby Champion, Loyola defeated Cincinnati in overtime to win the NCAA Basketball Championship, and Texas was the NCAA Football Champion with a perfect record. Other historical events of note that year included the first artificial heart transplant in a human by Dr. Michael E. De Bakey and the U.S. Supreme Court ruled that no locality may require recitation of the Lord's Prayer or Bible verses in public schools. And in the literary world *Vonnegut's Cat's Cradle, Updike's The Centaur, Schulz's Happiness is a Warm Puppy, Plath's The Bell Jar,* and *Baldwin's The Fire Next Time* were published.

What does any of this have to do with my story? Probably nothing, but you have to admit that there were some strange, sad, and even wonderful things going on in 1963 besides the events of the summer of my fourteenth year. Which brings me back to the story. Roger still wanted to be friends, but he DID NOT want to go with me to mow yards any more. Even though I labeled him 'Little Kelvin', we were still best buddies and had lots of fun that summer regardless of the strange things that had happened to me and would continue to happen until school started in August. I still had lots of money to make before school started back and most of my days were spent looking for yards to mow. And as Roger would find out, he didn't have to tag along with me to be involved in the strange happenings in my life.

Roger and I were out in the street after dinner on that Friday afternoon before my birthday tossing the football back and forth when Roger tossed it my way as if I were going out for a pass and the football stopped in mid-air about half way to me and dropped to the ground. I turned around and looked at Roger and he looked at me and I said, "What kind of girlie throw was that?"

"I didn't throw it any different than before," he said in defense. "It just stopped in mid-air and dropped to the ground."

"Yeh, right," I chided him. "You sneak in some kind of trick football?" I asked.

"No way, man!" he exclaimed. "It really did just drop out of mid-air."

We both walked toward the football to investigate this little trick further both thinking that the other was up to something. The one thing that hadn't occurred to us was that some mysterious force was at work here. Quite frankly, since nothing strange had happened for a couple of weeks we were feeling pretty comfortable with life. When we got to where the football had fallen in the street we stopped a couple of feet away from it, Roger on one side and me on the other, to stare at it for a minute. The strange thing was is that it hadn't rolled even a fraction of an inch when it hit the pavement and it was still fully inflated.

"Well, pick it up and let's see what's wrong with it," I almost commanded Roger.

"No way, dude," Roger came back at me with a tremble in his voice. "YOU pick it up first."

"What's to be afraid of, man?" I asked. "It's not going to bite you. Now pick it up."

Roger was definitely scared to pick it up and said, "I said NO WAY and I meant NO DANG WAY! It can lay there until the frigging cows come home before I pick it up!"

"Oh, for crying out loud!" I exclaimed and reached down to pick up the football. At that very moment a bolt of heat lightning flashed across the sky and the loudest clap of thunder I'd ever heard followed immediately after it. I think I must have jumped farther than Roger and we both fell backwards on our hind ends scooting back away from the football about ten feet, putting about twenty feet between us. We stared at each other wide-eyed and silent for what seemed like ten minutes, but was probably only a few seconds, and then looked toward where the football had been at the same time.

"Holy crap!" Roger exclaimed in a low, frightened voice. "Where's the frigging football?"

"It must have rolled away when it thundered," I tried to explain, not believing what I was saying. I looked around to see if I could find the football nearby in the gloom as it was getting to be darker and now there was a big dark storm cloud up above. "Maybe we should just call it a night and look for it tomorrow," I suggested since it wasn't my football.

"Sounds good to me," Roger said as we both got slowly up off the street still looking around for the football, or whatever might be lurking in the shadows. We turned, said goodnight, and slowly started to walk toward our houses. After about five or six steps we both simultaneously broke into a run and disappeared inside.

When I got inside I asked my dad, who was watching television, if he had heard that loud clap of thunder a few minutes ago. "Have you been listening to loud music again?" he asked. "It's clear as a bell out there so there couldn't have been any thunder and lightning. The weatherman on the television just said so. There's no chance for rain for at least four or five days. Which reminds me, you need to water your mother's flowers tomorrow morning before you do anything else."

"Yes, sir," I replied. "I'll be right back. I forgot to put something away outside," I said and headed back out the door to check the sky for that dark cloud. When I got to the end of the carport I cautiously peeked around the corner to make sure no one or no thing was there and then looked up at the sky. To both my surprise and horror the stars were shining brightly and there wasn't even a small white cloud anywhere close. Oh boy, I thought to myself. It's starting up again.

Chapter Seventeen

The next morning at the breakfast table my dad suggested that I take the day off from mowing yards and just bum out since the next day was my birthday. Mom agreed and said that I didn't even have to do any chores if I didn't want to. Well, that was a guilt trip of the third degree in disguise if I had ever heard one. She knew that I would at least wash, dry, and put away the breakfast dishes. My parents both left for work at their usual times and basically the day was mine to do whatever I wanted. Dad was going to take off from work tomorrow, however, for my birthday. I still liked to go fishing, especially salt-water fishing, and the plan was to pack the cooler with mom's fried chicken, homemade potato salad, and plenty of soft drinks (especially my favorite, Nehi Grape). We couldn't afford a boat or to pay to go deep sea fishing so Dad and I had two or three spots along one of the causeways where we knew we could catch redfish, snook, and the occasional snapper or flounder. Dad preferred shrimp and cut up squid for bait in salt water and he liked to fish the shady spots where mangroves grew along the shore. Once in a while we would stop on one of the bridges along the causeway and try to catch bigger snapper that way. We were lucky sometimes, but we didn't really have the equipment to fish in the deeper waters.

Well, as suspected, I cleaned up the breakfast dishes and crashed in front of the television to watch cartoons, because I wasn't quite ready to venture back outside just yet. My favorites were *Mighty Mouse*, *Rocky and Bullwinkle*, and *Popeye* (which was already in re-runs). I also liked to watch *The Lone Ranger*, which was also in re-runs since the last episode was first broadcast in 1957. I can remember back when I was five years old listening to *The Lone Ranger* on the radio (because we couldn't afford a television yet) that sat on the kitchen table at the back of the little shot-gun house my parents rented when we first moved to Florida. That was short lived, however, since the radio series ended in September of that year. I watched television until almost noon, getting up every thirty minutes to change the channel to see what was on the other two channels we got. I realized all of a sudden that I was getting hungry and that the eggs and grits and biscuits and sausage gravy we had for breakfast was beginning to wear off. It's hard work watching television all morning having to get up every thirty minutes to change the channels.

I got up and went to the kitchen to do my usual raid of the fridge and pantry when I was home alone around lunchtime. My first course was two peanut butter and jelly sandwiches. I could have eaten peanut butter and strawberry preserves spread thick between two slices of Sunbeam white bread for every meal if my mom would have let me. After I finished my sandwiches I decided to see what we had in the fridge for my second course. I knew there was some banana pudding left over from last night and that was sounding really good! I put my plate in the sink that I had used for my sandwiches and moseyed over to the fridge to get the pudding bowl out so I could dish me up a great big ol' bowl of mom's delicious banana pudding. I opened the fridge and pulled out the aluminum foil covered bowl, which felt a little light since it should still have had about half of the banana pudding left in it. You have to understand, this was no ordinary bowl. It was about 10 inches in diameter across the top and probably seven or eight inches deep. When mom made banana pudding she didn't fool around. That bowl would be full almost to the top with the most beautiful thick meringue with golden brown tips that you have ever seen and between my dad and me it would last about two days.

I placed the heavy bowl on the counter and removed the foil to find it EMPTY! *EMPTY!* Now, if that wasn't bad enough since I had my taste buds all set for a big ol' bowl of banana pudding, there was the fact that the bowl was EMPTY! Mom might have put some in Dad's lunch and even if it hadn't had as much in the bowl as I thought it did, Mom would NEVER have put the bowl back in the fridge empty. And Dad would never fix his own lunch—that was what a wife did for her working husband—so he didn't put the bowl back in the fridge empty. I carefully picked up the aluminum foil to examine it, because mom had put a new piece over the bowl last night. I had been very careful in removing the aluminum foil, because in my sneaky ways I guess I thought that if I removed it carefully and replaced it carefully and only took one bowl that mom wouldn't know the difference (just goes to show how naïve a nearly fourteen year old boy can be). My inspection indicated to me that I was obviously the first to remove this particular piece of aluminum foil from this particular bowl since it had been placed there the night before by my mom. Now, if THIS wasn't bad enough on top of the fact that I still had a craving for some banana pudding, HOW was I going to explain the empty bowl that had been half full to my mom when she got home from work? Just tell the truth you say. Tell her that the bowl was already empty when I took it out of the fridge. *Yeh, right! Like she would buy into that!*

Since there wasn't anything I could do about the empty bowl I thought I would just carefully put the aluminum foil back on the bowl and return it to the fridge. When she pulled it out after dinner to dish up some for dad and me and discovered that it was empty she might just think that she put it in the fridge that way and that it had been a couple of days since she made it. It was a long shot, but it was all I had, so the empty banana pudding bowl with the aluminum foil carefully placed back on top went back in the fridge in exactly the same spot where it had been.

This little event got me to thinking about the night before and the lightning incident and all of a sudden I lost my appetite. Could the old hag or the old man or Mom number two or one of the reptilian alien things or some other horrible creature be hiding in the house and had snuck into the kitchen while I was watching cartoons and eaten all of the banana pudding? The up side of that was that whatever it was that had eaten the banana pudding hadn't slipped up behind me in the living room while I was watching television and killed and eaten me. Or worse, eaten me alive! *HOLY JUMPING BULLFROGS*, I thought to myself! *I had better get outside where I had some running room before whoever or WHATEVER that was lurking somewhere in the house comes out and gets me! I bet that whatever was hiding in my house was probably hiding in the bathtub behind the shower curtain in our one and only bathroom waiting for me to come in to take a leak. It would jump out and grab me in mid-pee with my wanky hanging out and pull me back into the tub with the shower curtain closed and eat me there. That way it could wash the blood down the drain and the police would never be the wiser. The newspaper headline would read, NEARLY FOURTEEN YEAR OLD LOCAL BOY DISAPPEARS INTO THIN AIR AFTER GORGING ON BANANA PUDDING! POLICE ARE STUMPED AND CRAVING SOME BANANA PUDDING!*

I almost started to go to the bathroom because all of a sudden I had to pee. *OH NO*, I thought to myself, *you can't lure me into the bathroom with your mind games. I don't really have to pee, whatever you are is making me think that I have to pee.* With that thought I was out the kitchen door in a flash and got my bicycle out of the storage room and positioned it at the end of the carport facing the street for a quick getaway if the thing came out the door after me. The Kiches' Rambler was gone and for once I wished that it had been there. As much as I hated Kelvin and especially hated his tattletale mother, I would have gladly welcomed their presence right now. I looked up and down the street and across the street to Roger's house and there wasn't a soul in sight anywhere. There weren't any cars in any of the driveways. There weren't any garages in our neighborhood, because people who lived in this part of town couldn't afford a house with a garage. *Could the thing that was now inside my house have already been at work on my street and done away with everyone who lived there?*

I wasn't hanging around to find out so I jumped on my bicycle and took off down the driveway, because I wanted to get as far away from my house right now as I could. Just as I reached the end of the driveway my bicycle seemed to hit an invisible wall, because it stopped abruptly and I went flying over the handlebars and landed in the middle of the dirt street. That was one time I was glad that they hadn't paved our street yet. It probably wouldn't get paved anytime soon either, because our neighborhood wasn't very important to city government. For a few seconds I just lay there in the dirt stunned. *What the heck had just happened? Had my brakes locked up all by themselves sending me over the handlebars? Was the evil thing that was in my house now outside and invisible and had it grabbed my bicycle from behind causing me to end up in the street?*

"Help me, Jesus," I muttered out loud. "Please don't let this thing get me and eat me," I pleaded to Jesus or anyone who might be in hearing range.

"What has gotten into you, youngin?" a voice said from behind me, making me turn and jump about three feet in the opposite direction at the same time. I looked up and into the face of Mrs. Chyspo, who lived six houses down the street from us and was out walking her tiny little Papillion dog named Bamboo. "You tryin to kill yourself on that bicycle?" she asked.

"No, ma'am," I replied. "I don't know what happened. All of a sudden my brakes must have locked up and I went flying over the handle bars."

"Well, are you hurt?" she asked me, seemingly concerned.

"I don't think so," I replied trying to look at myself everywhere to see if I was bleeding anywhere.

"Are your parents home?" she asked.

"No, ma'am. They're both at work," I replied without thinking about why she would be asking me that.

"Well, why don't you come on down to my house and we'll get you all cleaned up," she said as if that was what she always did in life, clean accident prone little kids up.

"Sure," I eagerly agreed knowing that I certainly didn't want to go back in my house right now.

I picked myself and my bicycle up and walked down the street with Mrs. Chyspo to her house with little Bamboo briskly walking along side. When we got to her house she unlocked her front door, ushered me inside, undid Bamboo's leash from her collar, and locked the door back. That should have been my first clue since I had missed the others.

Chapter Eighteen

The first clue was Mrs. Chyspo suddenly appearing out of nowhere when there hadn't been ANYONE ANYWHERE up and down the street! The second clue was her asking me if I was trying to kill myself (before, that is, she or whoever was posing as her had a chance to do it!)! The third was asking me if I was hurt, because she obviously didn't want to eat damaged goods! Well, it was TOO late now to be thinking about all these things I hadn't thought about when I should have been thinking instead of worrying if I had a scratch on me! But then that was no doubt part of her plan: discombobulate me by making my bicycle come to a screeching halt so that I would go flying over the handle bars and land on my back in the dirt! Of course I wasn't hurt, that was all part of the plan. As a matter of fact, I didn't even remember hitting the ground, which means that she used her magic powers to cushion my fall. And now she had tricked me into coming into Mrs. Chyspo's house, because this couldn't possibly be the real Mrs. Chyspo, and she had locked the door and was standing in the way so that I couldn't exit.

"I think that I should go home and clean up, Mrs. Chyspo," I practically pleaded.

"Oh, I don't think so, youngin," she said in a strange low voice that obviously did not belong to Mrs. Chyspo. "I think you are going to the kitchen and wash the dirt off in there close to the oven."

"I'm not going anywhere but home," I replied in as convincing a voice as I could.

At that precise moment whatever it was that was posing as Mrs. Chyspo starting turning into the reptilian alien with the big mouth and long teeth. I backed up about three steps before running into something soft and fleshy feeling against my back. I was almost too scared to turn around to see what I had bumped into for fear that the reptilian alien thing would eat me up in one gulp as soon as my back was turned! However, my curiosity won out and I swung around rapidly thinking that I would make a quick complete circle and come back face to face with the horrible thing that was getting ready to have me for lunch. What I didn't expect the soft fleshiness to be was Monica standing there in a skimpy bikini with her arms outstretched to give me a big hug! Well, needless to say, but I will anyway because I was a nearly-fourteen-year-old boy with raging hormones, my eyes got big and I froze in my turn with my back to the creature that was no doubt closing in on its lunch!

"Monica, I love you! Help me!" I screamed!

"Quick, hon, get behind me!" she screamed back at me and grabbed my arm pulling me around behind her, where I might add the view wasn't bad either!

I peeked around her to see if the monster was still advancing toward us, but there wasn't a monster or Mrs. Chyspo with her dog or an old hag or an old man. There was just an empty room and an open door. Monica turned to face me and her breasts brushed against my chest and I thought I was going to faint. She reached out and took hold of my arms and pulled me to her, wrapping her arms around me and giving me a big hug and pressing her gorgeous breasts into my skinny little chest. Remembering that I was a nearly-fourteen-year-old boy I can tell you that the raging hormones were all headed to the same place!

Monica pushed me back but held on to my arms and said, "You're all mine now, little darlin."

I tried to say GREAT, but nothing but a low moan came out of my mouth and then I realized that her fingernails were digging deeper into my arms and it was starting to hurt. Instead, I said, "Monica, you're hurting me. Let go. Please."

"I don't think so little darlin," she cooed as her skin began to look darker and started to wrinkle up. I swung my arms upward between her arms and back down on her arms as hard as a ninety pound weakling could. Her hold broke and I shoved her hard backward and scampered around her left side toward the open door. I later thought that I did that because that was probably her weaker side. I was almost to the open door when it slammed shut all by itself. Of course it didn't slam on its own, it was part of the old hag's magic that made it slam shut. I turned quickly back around to face the old hag only to find the room completely empty and a strange and scary laughing coming from out of the walls close to where the old hag had been standing.

I turned back toward the door and ran up to it grabbing the door knob and turning it and pulling hard expecting the door to be stuck shut. Instead the door swung open freely causing me to almost fall backward. I regained my balance and darted out the door faster than I ever remembered being able to run.

Where was I going to run? I wasn't thinking about that at the moment and was back in my driveway before I remembered that something was probably waiting for me inside. The other thing that occurred to me at that moment was that my bicycle was back in Mrs. Chyspo's living room. How would I explain that to my parents? I could always claim that it was stolen, but my explanations (or lies, if you prefer) were rarely convincing. If I told them that it was inside Mrs. Chyspo's house they would say if that was true then I needed to go get it. And when I got back I would have to come up with an explanation as to how it got inside her house in the first place.

Then I looked toward the back of the carport next to the storage shed and there was my bicycle. *What the heck was going on? Had I imagined everything after my bicycle accident and unconsciously put my bicycle up and ended up standing in the middle of our driveway not knowing what was really going on? Had I really had a bicycle accident? Maybe I really am going insane.* I didn't remember mowing down any funny mushrooms lately, not that I even knew what they looked like. Maybe turning fourteen meant that you started losing your mind! I often thought that adults, especially my parents, had lost their minds, but then most teenagers probably think that about adults.

Well, there was one thing for sure: I wasn't going back in my house and I wasn't going out into the street, so I decided to sit right down there in the middle of the driveway and wait for my parents to get home. Of course, that was based on the belief that they really were my parents.

Chapter Nineteen

Now that was the scariest thought I had had all day! Had I really been living with aliens all these years who were just waiting for me to ripen! Was fourteen years old the "just right" age for devouring human young that they had abducted from their real human parents when they were still babies. That couldn't possibly be true could it? I mean, my parents moved to central Florida from Alabama and there couldn't possibly be aliens in Alabama! Remember, my dad had said that he didn't want me growing up in a city like Birmingham with all that crime. Or did they move to this little town in Florida because as aliens they might have been found out easier in a larger place? And if my parents really were aliens wouldn't they have been trying to fatten me up for the "coming of ripe age" feast on my fourteenth birthday instead of letting me stay so skinny all my life? Of course, my size might be genetic like we learned in science class back in the seventh grade and my alien parents wouldn't have known that when they abducted me as a baby. But if they were aliens and had come to earth from some planet in a distant galaxy wouldn't they be smart enough to figure such things out by running some sort of test on the babies first? And did my alien parents take on the look of my real parents after killing and possibly even eating them or did they just look around and find the most common-looking people they could find to change into to be my parents. Ok, so maybe that was cruel, but my parents weren't exactly the embodiment of what was considered beautiful, which for the first time in my life made me realize that I wasn't going to grow up to be all that good-looking either.

Back to the fear at hand; tomorrow was my fourteenth birthday and I was going out of town on a fishing trip to Tampa with my parents. *Was this their alien scheme to get me off in an isolated place away from home where I could disappear and the police report would just be stamped "MISSING" and the newspaper headlines in both towns would read, FOURTEEN YEAR OLD BOY DISAPPEARS FROM CAUSEWAY. PICNIC LUNCH UNEATEN, BUT PARENTS LOOKED STUFFED!* About the time this thought ran through my head I heard someone ask me why I was sitting in the driveway in the heat. I looked up to see my mom standing over me and I said, "I was out riding my bicycle and when I got back and was going to put it up I thought I heard something or someone in the house and I got scared again and decided to wait out here until you and dad got home."

"You and your ghosts," mom said. "What are we going to do with you?" That was probably about the millionth time I had heard that in my life, but this was the first time that it scared the heebie-jeebies out of me!

"Guess you'll just have to love me forever," I said hoping that would help to convince her not to kill and eat me tomorrow on our fishing trip.

"Well, of course we will, dear," she replied in that motherly voice of love and compassion. "Now, let's go in and make sure the house is safe for habitation."

Habitation, I thought. My real mom had never used that word in all the years that my mind could remember. That had to be a clue, but I really didn't have any choice but to go in the house with this woman who certainly looked like my mom and surely she wouldn't jump the gun and have me for dinner before I turned fourteen. And besides, what if the man who looked like my dad came home expecting something else for dinner to find out that his mate had had me for dinner and not left him anything? Mom and I went inside to find the house empty, of course, and as soon as we had explored every room, including behind the shower curtain, we started preparing dinner for when dad got home. It was about an hour later when Dad finally got home and Mom had to reheat his dinner. Mom and I had already eaten because she didn't want me to eat a cold or reheated dinner. *Consideration for my well-being or was a hot meal more fattening than a cold or reheated one?* A teenage boy who was "coming of ripe age" had to think about these things. Of course, Dad's first comment when he came in was to ask why my bicycle was still sitting out in the carport propped against the wall. Without saying a word I went outside to put it in the storage shed. When I had it tucked away in its proper place in the shed--Dad had a place for everything—and locked the shed door I turned around to come face to face with Kelvin. How had that big fairy snuck up behind me so quietly? He must have been hiding behind their Rambler.

"Well, well, well, hot shot," he said in that I'm going to kick your ass voice, "you sure have been causing a lot of trouble for me and my mother."

"Any trouble you have you caused for yourself," I suggested more than stated.

"You little turd," Kelvin whispered so no one would hear him. "I'm going to kick your butt!" he said a little louder now that he was getting riled up. "First time I catch you off your property I'll squish you like a tomato!"

Getting my nerve up a little and giggling I said, "You could certainly squish anything just by sitting on it. Only problem is you probably couldn't get your fat butt up off your sofa long enough to even go outside without your mommy going with you and neither one of you can run fast enough to catch a dead turtle much less me." By now I was laughing so hard I had a hard time standing up.

"You're dead meat, butthole," Kelvin nearly screamed as he lunged at me with a right hook. Now, I had backed up against the storage room wall because Kelvin kept moving toward me as we had our little discussion, he weighing about three times more than me. He could probably have pushed their Rambler by simply pushing his fat gut against it. That thought made me giggle even more as he was swinging at me. However, being faster on my feet than Kelvin I both ducked and moved quickly to my right and his big fat fist rammed hard into the wooden side of the storage shed. I quickly opened the kitchen door and slipped inside. When I had closed and locked the door I peeked out through the window curtain, that Mom had made herself, to see Kelvin bumping into and across the front of our car and falling down in the grass between our driveways holding his right hand with his left hand and crying. Kelvin was crying! Big, mean, tough Kelvin was crying! I'm sure you are probably thinking, "Aw, poor Kelvin," but this sight was even funnier to me at the time and I was now rolling on the floor laughing so hard that my eyes were beginning to water.

Dad had finished his dinner and was in the living room watching television, but my commotion in the kitchen made him actually get up out of his easy chair and come into the kitchen to see what was going on. When he asked me what was so funny all I could do was point at the window. He peeked out to see Kelvin still writhing on the ground crying even louder and still clutching his right hand. Dad turned back to me trying to hide the grin creeping across his lips, but it was no use. He was even laughing a little when he asked me what had happened. I tried to stop laughing so hard and managed to tell him what had transpired just outside our door. When I had finished, Dad, too, was actually laughing. My mom had been in the bedroom folding and putting away underwear when she came out into the kitchen and wanted to know what was so funny. Dad related the story to her and for one of the few times in my life, Mom actually laughed out loud.

After we finally settled down, dad peeked out again to see that Kelvin was no longer outside. "Probably had been rescued by his mommy," Dad suggested. That got all three of us laughing again. We all settled down at the dinner table and mom got the banana pudding out of the fridge and we each had a big bowl. After that we all retired to the living room to watch television, which was one of the very few times that we were all watching television together when I was a teenager. I had actually forgotten the bad events of the day and was beginning to look forward to the fishing trip on my birthday.

Chapter Twenty

Dad had us up around five on that Sunday morning, July 21, 1963. I was now officially fourteen years old. FOURTEEN FRIGGING YEARS OLD! In two short years I would be buying my first car even though I didn't know at that time how awful that car was going to be. And I was too excited at the time to realize that the next two years weren't going to be any shorter than the last two years or the two years before that.

Dad and I loaded the fishing gear into the trunk of our 1957 two-tone tropical coral and glacier white four door swept-wing Dodge Royal Lancer that he had found about a year ago at the savings and loan where he went to get a small loan to actually buy a car. This one had been repossessed and all he had to do was take over the payments on the car. Mom and I both loved the car, especially the coral and white colors, the dual headlights, and the wide white side wall tires. I especially liked the 325 cubic inch V-8 engine and the three-speed push-button automatic transmission. I would have been very happy to have had this car "handed down" to me when I turned sixteen if Dad hadn't traded it about a year from then for a 1959 Chrysler Imperial. That car was a little too fancy for my liking, but it did have a 413 cubic inch power plant and was a very comfortable ride. Dad never seemed to be satisfied with the car we had for more than two years at a time, a trait that he unfortunately passed on to me.

Back to getting ready for the fishing trip to Tampa, Mom had prepared fried chicken the night before that we would eat cold along with some homemade potato salad and banana pudding for dessert. This was all packed into a large cooler along with soft drinks, especially Grape Nehi for me since it was my birthday, and then covered with ice bought at the bait shop where we stopped on the way out of town. We didn't buy any bait there because dad liked to get fresher bait closer to where we would be fishing and the fact that you just couldn't buy cut squid and live greenback shiners for fishing in central Florida. After a great breakfast of hotcakes with warm Log Cabin Syrup (my favorite all time syrup, Aunt Jemima, wouldn't come along for another three years) and crisp bacon, we loaded ourselves into the Dodge, pulled out of the driveway and headed off toward Tampa. Dad liked to drive the back route, Highway 92, to Tampa because all of Interstate Four wasn't completed yet in the Tampa area and, besides, people just "drove way too fast out on the highway."

About an hour later we drove out onto the causeway and decided to pull off at the first of Dad's favorite fishing spots. He said this was a good spot because you could see the water moving as the tide was changing, but we had better hurry and get our lines in the water or we'd miss all the fish. It was already close to seven o'clock and dad was fussing about not getting there early enough to catch the best fish (he preferred to get to his favorite fishing holes before sunrise). But Mom told him to quit fussing because it was my birthday and maybe I didn't really want to go fishing in the first place. Of course I wanted to go fishing I reassured Dad and today I would catch the biggest fish ever!

Dad and I unloaded the fishing gear from the trunk and Mom set up three lawn chairs close to the water. Mom liked to fish sometimes, but today she just wanted to watch. Dad and I baited our hooks with live greenback shiners, probably snooks' favorite food, and cast our lines out into the water, sat down in our lawn chairs, and waited for something to come along and take the bait. About ten minutes passed when something started pulling on my line and I grabbed up my rod and reel and started to play whatever was at the other end. When whatever it was had taken out about ten feet of line, Dad said to pull back hard on the rod, which I did, and whatever was at the other end obviously didn't like it because my rod was nearly jerked out of my hands as whatever was out there pulled hard in the other direction. I pulled back hard on the rod and turned the handle on my reel three or four times to take up some line. The rod bent double back toward the water and I pulled hard back and reeled in some more line against whatever had decided that it liked my particular shiner. This little battle went on for about another ten minutes with my dad getting more and more excited about what I had hooked and telling me over and over again to play it. It was about this time that we saw it really was a fish, A BIG FISH, because it broke the shallow water, jumped and made a huge splash as it fell back into the water. Dad yelled that it was a snook, A BIG ONE, and grabbed up the long-handled net and waded out into the water to help me pull it in. I hadn't noticed, but Mom was standing behind me with her hands clasped in front of her and telling me over and over not to lose it. I kept reeling it in with everything I had in my skinny little arms and Dad finally got it into the net, which barely held it. He quickly walked back to the shore and carried it up away from the water. This one wasn't getting away and he was making sure. He told mom to get the tape measure out of the car while he tried to get it untangled from the fishing net. It was still flopping around all over the place when she came back with the tape measure, but dad put his big size twelve left foot down on it and got an approximate measure of twenty-nine inches, which wasn't far off. We re-measured it when we got it home and it turned out to actually be close to thirty inches long and felt like it weighed a hundred pounds. Of course it didn't weigh anywhere near that much, but I never did know how much it actually weighed because Dad didn't have a fish scale. Dad did say that he thought it was probably around eight pounds since it was a gulf snook. He had heard that Atlantic snook usually weighed a little more so that was why he was guessing that this one weighed about eight pounds. However, I had caught the biggest fish ever, for me, and it was even bigger than anything Dad had ever caught in salt water. Dad wasn't sure whether or not it was legal to keep snook at that time of the year or what the minimum size was if there was a minimum size, but we put it in the second cooler, which only had ice in it, and took it home anyway. We would be eating some mighty tasty fish for a couple of days off this rascal. Mom would fry up the filets and make some hot buttered grits, creamy coleslaw and fresh biscuits hot from the oven to go along with it.

The rest of the morning was pretty slow with us catching a few small fish that we mostly threw back. All we could talk about was my snook and how tasty it was going to be that night at dinner. It was nearly noon before Dad decided that it was time for lunch and that was more out of consideration for Mom and me than himself. If he had his way when he was fishing he would fish all day without eating anything and sometimes never move from one fishing hole, even if he wasn't catching anything. I asked him one time how he could just sit there for long periods of time when the fish weren't biting. He told me that when he went fishing it was his time and sometimes he just liked to be outdoors where he could think about unimportant things and not have to worry about earning money and paying bills. Unfortunately, Dad only got to go fishing about once a month on a Sunday morning, because he had to work most Sundays just to keep us one step ahead of the bill collectors.

After lunch we packed up and drove a few miles to another location where we had to walk back onto a low bridge where the water on one side of the causeway was always flowing swiftly under the bridge to the other side of the causeway. Dad believed that when fishing in salt water it was better for catching fish if the water was moving. We walked about half way out on the bridge giving the other two fishermen who were out there plenty of room so our lines wouldn't get tangled up together. Dad and I moved about ten feet apart for the same reason and dropped our lines into the swiftly moving water. We were on the side of the bridge where the water was running under the bridge instead of away from it. One other fisherman was on the other side of the bridge. Dad said that the biggest fish liked to be in the shade under the bridge and maybe we would have some luck before we headed home.

About thirty minutes had passed and we hadn't even had one little nibble and from the look of things the other three fishermen weren't having any luck either. Over the next thirty minutes or so all three of the other fishermen left one at a time wishing the remaining fishermen good luck. Dad said that if we didn't catch something soon we would head back home and just feast on my fish. That was starting to sound like a really good idea to me when there were three quick, hard jerks on my rod that, once again, almost pulled it out of my hands. If I hadn't been reeling my line in to try a different spot I would probably have lost rod and reel right there. I let out a "Holy crap!" which made dad look up with a jerk of his head. When he saw I was struggling against something with my rod and barely hanging on to it he dropped his rod and ran over to help me.

"Whatcha got there, son?, he said excitedly.
"I . . . don't . . . know . . . , but . . . it's . . . bigger . . . than . . . the . . . other . . . one," I said struggling hard to not lose my rod and reel over the side of the bridge. I was already hanging over the side because I had been caught off guard. Dad reached for my rod and reel and I turned it over to him as soon as I knew he had a good grip on it. He pulled up hard on it and the rod bent over double and even though he had a firm

grip on the reel handle I could hear the line screeching off the reel anyway.

"Holy crap!" Dad exclaimed echoing my sentiments. "We may have to cut the line on this one. I don't think I can reel him in. Son of a gun, that's got to be a monster!" All I could do was stand by and watch as dad kept trying to reel in whatever it was that was on the other end of my line. Mom had heard the commotion and come running out on the bridge to see if everything was ok.

"Cut the line, Thurman, cut the line before you lose the rod or worse it pulls you in!" mom yelled at dad.

"Get the knife out of the tackle box, son," Dad told me. "Quick!" I ran back to the tackle box which had been near where dad had been fishing and got his knife out and ran back just as the line went slack on the rod and dad stood up straight with a jerk. "What the devil!" he exclaimed. We all three bent over the railing and looked down into the water expecting to see nothing more than a dangling piece of line. However, much to our shock we saw a fin moving through the water in the other direction. It had to be a small sand shark, probably about five feet long with the other end of my line coming from the vicinity of its mouth. It would only be a few seconds before it would be pulling on my line again. We always used a pretty strong line when we went saltwater fishing and that was probably why it hadn't broke yet. Dad also figured later that the hook had been imbedded pretty deep into the shark's mouth or it would have ripped out. Well, Dad grabbed the open knife and cut the line just as it was beginning to tighten up again and my biggest catch ever swam on out into deep water. That little adventure pretty much brought the day of fishing to a close and so we packed up and headed home with two good fish stories to tell and one good fish to eat!

Chapter Twenty-one

Monday morning, July 22, 1963, and things were back to normal as Mom was off to work, but, as Dad had promised, he was going to take me down to the Highway Patrol Station to get my learner's permit. Nothing very exciting to tell here as everything went along smoothly and I even got to drive back home. Dad had been teaching me to drive for the past year. We would occasionally go over to the old airstrip behind the baseball stadium and he would let me practice there. I would practice driving straight, backing up, turning left and right, parallel parking, and anything else that he thought I should know. You don't know just how bad I wanted to peel out in the '57 Dodge, but if I had Dad wouldn't have let me drive again until I was thirty! We got back home and Dad dropped me off at the house. He asked if I was going to try and find some more yards to mow that day and I assured him I would get my bicycle and the mower out and head out soon. Things had gone so smoothly on my birthday that I wasn't even thinking about all the horrible things I had been through thus far that summer. I got the lawn mower out first, then my bicycle and tied the mower to the back and then bravely headed back into one of the old neighborhoods where I had been mowing yards.

I didn't make this decision lightly or without thinking about it for the past 24 hours. I was actually thinking about it all day on my birthday though the fishing had taken my mind off it for a little while. My logic was that I got through my birthday without any unusual occurrences and so I figured that the old hag, the old man, reptilian lizard alien things, and Monica weren't interested in me anymore since they hadn't been able to do me in before or on my birthday. Besides, I was fourteen now, not just a year older, but a year braver. This was some weird theory I had come up with which stated that with each year that one grew older one also grew braver. I can tell you now that that proved to be a pretty naïve theory over the next several years.

There was once when I was fifteen and a really cute girl at school suggested that I come over to her house after school because her parents wouldn't be home and we could make out. Being the naïve virgin that I was who had never made out anything more than a few constellations in the night sky, I made up about six excuses as to why I couldn't go over to her house on that particular afternoon, except for the fact that I had never made out with anyone, and turned and ran like a scared rabbit as fast as I could to get to algebra class. Needless to say she never asked me again.

There was the time when I was sixteen, remember I had my own car then (a '59 Studebaker, woo, woo!), and was out cruising early one afternoon in the rain driving toward town on a one-way street when the old fart ahead of me decides to come to a complete stop at a green traffic light (you know, the color that means go, not stop). Well, I hit my brakes just about a nanosecond too late and gently bumped into him. There was obviously no damage, but as soon as he saw that some young punk had rear-ended his brand new 1965 Chevy Nova he decided to cause trouble. He started to get out of his car in the rain, but I rolled my window down and yelled for us to move our cars out of the street and over to the parking lot across the way. He waved ok, got back in his car and drove to the parking lot I had indicated. Well, my plan was working fine. Not only was I scared to face the old coot, but no doubt my dad would find out about this and he wouldn't let me drive until I turned forty! So this teenage boy who hadn't been driving very long floored it just as the old man was turning into the parking lot and once again ran like a scared rabbit, only this time I was driving and didn't have algebra class to use as an excuse. Since the old guy didn't try to follow me and the police never came to my house looking for the outlaw (alias, Jimmy the Kid) who had rear-ended the old man with his hot rod Studebaker I figured being scared got me off the hook once again.

These were certainly not the only times that running scared got me out of predicaments for the next several years, but they are fairly classic examples of how guys don't get braver as they get older, they just let their stupid pride get in their way sometimes and they try to act braver.

Well, again I digress, so back to my story for that eventful day after my birthday in 1963, the day that I was going to be brave (or totally stupid)! The first house I stopped at was where Mrs. Root Beer Lady lived, had lived, was hiding out, whatever the case had been, was now, and might forever be. I bravely sauntered up to the front door and knocked loudly. A few seconds passed and the door opened to reveal Mrs. Root Beer Lady! She looked exactly like she did the first time I ever saw her. She was even wearing the same housecoat and slippers. A quick peek inside also revealed the same old house and same old furniture and same old pictures that had been there the first time. Nothing had changed!

"Well, looky who's here! She delightedly exclaimed. "If it isn't my long-lost lawn boy. I thought you had forgotten about this old woman and was never coming back to mow my yard again. Why, I even figured you didn't like my cookies and rut beer any more. I'd made sumthin different if'ns you'd just said you didn't like my cookies and rut beer."

I thought she would ramble on forever, but she stopped right there and looked at me with hurt in her eyes. "No, ma'am," I replied. "I've just been so busy and my dad got me all these yards to mow in another part of town that I just haven't had time to get back over here, but I'll be glad to mow your yard today if you like."

"Why that would do my old heart so much good," she replied as she beamed at me.

"I'll get right on it," I said and turned to get my mower untied from my bicycle and get busy.

"Don't ferget yer cookies and rut beer after ye finish," she hollered after me.

"I won't," I assured her as best I could. Well, seems like the old gal was just as nice as in the beginning. Maybe I had been dreaming or hallucinating all those horrible confrontations with her. I got busy and finished the yard in record time. I was becoming such a pro at mowing yards these days what with all the practice I was getting. When I had finished I went back to her front door and was about to knock when I remembered way back when she had scolded me for knocking and not just coming on in. So, I just opened the door and strode in like the place belonged to me. She must have heard me and called me back to the kitchen where chocolate chip cookies and root beer were waiting for me on the kitchen table.

"Do you like my new kitchen table?" she asked.

I looked it over quickly, but closely, and it looked just like the one she had before, right down to the dings on the corners and the scratches on the legs.

"It's real nice," I said. "Looks kind of like the one you had before."

"You stupid little scatter brained hoodlum!" she exclaimed in that deep voice I had heard a couple of times before. "It's the same dang table, you rotten little turd!"

Starting to go against my theory of getting braver as one aged, I said with a quiver in my voice, "I thought it looked familiar."

"Lie, lie, lie! That's all you little hoodlums can do, ain't it?" she stated more than asked in an even deeper voice now. "Lying is how you youngins manage to get out of all kinds of trouble and fool old people into believing all kinds of untruths. Why, I bet yer ain't even looked at that nice Bible I give yer. The Devil himself is goin ta rise up one day and devour you like so much bait on a fishin hook, exceptin He ain't goona get caught like that poor snook you and yer parents devoured for dinner last night!"

Ok, what was the first clue I once again overlooked that got me into another bad situation with this old hag, this witch who obviously had the power to see and know all? Something deep inside of me flashed this little message across my pea sized brain in a split second, but long enough for me to take it in and act: *"WORRYING ABOUT CLUES ARE YOU? AND THE WITCH IS GETTING READY TO EAT YOU!"* I quickly assessed my situation and position to figure out what my easiest and fastest way out would be. I could try to get out the back door, which was the closest means of escape, but I would have to get past the old hag who was standing between the door and me. I could turn and run back through the house and out the front door, but that might give her time to catch me. I knew from past experiences that she was faster than most people would think. My choice was turn and run faster than a scared rabbit back through the house, out the front door, jump onto my bicycle, and once again pedal for my life. I had tied the mower up to the bicycle before I came in because somewhere in the back of my mind I still had my doubts about this old woman.

I turned and took off through the door into the kitchen from the other room and ran around and jumped over furniture heading toward the front door. But one small problem popped up: THERE WASN'T A DOOR IN THE ROOM! Not where I thought I had come into the house, not at either end of the room, and as I turned around swiftly to go back through the door into the kitchen I came to a grinding stop in the middle of the living room. Yes, there was a door back into the kitchen, but the old hag was occupying that space and grinning from ear to ear; really, her grin was stretching all the way from one ear to the other and a mouthful of shark-like teeth were gleaming at me in the dim light of the living room. The opening of her mouth started growing bigger and bigger and the shark-like teeth were growing bigger right along with it. She, it, or whatever this thing was started moving toward me obviously with lunch on its mind. Only it was moving rather slowly as if this physical change was slowing it down. I took this as an opportunity to out maneuver the creature that the old hag had turned into and sprinted to my right jumping over two end tables and knocking over a floor lamp in the process. The creature with the ever enlarging mouth full of shark-like teeth had moved slowly into the room about six paces and this gave me enough room to scamper through the door into the kitchen and out the back door, which she had obviously forgotten to seal up with a wall like she did in the living room. This time I was running faster than I had ever run in my life and ran around the right side of the house and toward the front yard. As I passed the front corner of the house I looked to see if the thing that had been Mrs. Root Beer Lady just moments ago was coming out the front door trying to catch up to me. To my surprise there still wasn't an opening in the front of the house where the door had been and no one or no thing was coming out after me. I jumped on my bicycle and pedaled faster than I thought I was capable heading back the way I had come. Once again it seemed that I had escaped the clutches of the old hag.

Chapter Twenty-two

As I pedaled as fast as I could with a lawn mower in tow up the street I had no idea where I was heading, but I did know that I wasn't going to stop until I had put at least a couple of miles between me and where I had just escaped. I don't think that I was really thinking about where I was heading, but when I had to stop because I was out of breath and I thought my legs were going to fall off I was sitting in front of Monica's house. This had to be some psychological trick that the old hag or the old man or even Monica was playing on my mind.

What I wanted to do at this moment was run up to Monica's door and see if that knock-dead gorgeous blond would answer the door and once again take me into her arms and press me against her ample breasts, giving me refuge from the evil that seemed to follow me around wherever I went. Now, my older, more adult, braver, and more intelligent mind should have told me to stay as far away from this house as possible, but fourteen year old male hormones tend to take precedence over all of those other things. That being the case I did what my body, not my mind, was telling me to do and ran toward Monica's house to find the sweet soft comfort of those ample breasts. I just knew that she would be waiting for me just behind that front door, not because of the psychic communication between her and the old hag, but because she couldn't wait to hold me and caress me. I didn't even bother to knock, again knowing in my heart that the door would be unlocked, and so I turned the knob and rushed into the living room of the house. I quickly closed the door and locked it before I turned around to let Monica comfort me against her ample breasts. Have I mentioned that she had ample breasts?

When I turned around there wasn't any Monica waiting to comfort me. As a matter of fact, there wasn't anyone waiting to comfort me or eat me or scare me half to death. The room was empty. I mean EMPTY! No Monica, no old hag, no old man, no furniture, NOTHING! I looked around the room and into the next rooms from where I was standing and didn't notice any furniture or anything else anywhere. Even though this was a little scary I decided to investigate the other rooms beginning with the kitchen, which was in the same location in this house as the one in the old hag's house. I cautiously peeked into the kitchen to find the same situation there: no furniture, people, or creatures hungry for a teenage boy lunch. I continued my investigation into the two bedrooms, where I secretly hoped to find Monica waiting for me, and the one bathroom to find a completely empty house. Except for two things: there were very dark, possibly black, curtains over all of the windows and the lights were all on. Maybe I was becoming more observant in my old age since I probably wouldn't have noticed these things before or maybe I was just getting used to looking for things out of the ordinary. I was pretty sure that Monica had had pretty pink ruffled curtains before – I hoped that none of my buddies ever found out that I had noticed or even thought about "pretty pink curtains" – *so why were there now black curtains hanging in her house? And why would someone have left the lights on?*

I was standing back in the center of what had one time been Monica's living room when I heard something that sounded like a long skirt swishing across the floor. I quickly did a 360 turn to discover that the room was still empty. As the swishing became louder I then noticed it was because the curtains, which lightly touched the floor, were gently moving back and forth as if there was a breeze around the baseboards or the windows were open. I knew the windows weren't open because of the temperature in the house. It must have been 110 degrees inside. Then all of a sudden the

lights all went out at the same time and the temperature must have dropped to freezing and the curtains
quit moving. Even though it was almost noon and the
sun was almost directly overhead, it was pitch black
dark in the house and very cold. I couldn't even see
my hand in front of my face. I was once again scared
to death and just knew that something would jump out
of the dark and grab me so I wasn't even breathing,
much less moving figuring that whatever was going to
jump out of the dark and grab me would have a harder
time finding me if I didn't breathe or move. Only problem was that I was asthmatic and couldn't hold my
breath very long, so after about thirty seconds I
gasped hard for air and bent over in the process.
Lucky for me that I did bend over because as I did
something went swoosh over me and crashed into one
of the walls. It was still pitch black dark so I couldn't
see what had crashed into the wall or even which wall
it had crashed into. I fell to my hands and knees thinking that I might have a better chance at finding a door
and escaping if I were crawling. Then I heard whatever had flown over me and crashed start moving and it
sounded like it was moving toward me since the shuf-
fling sound was slowly getting louder. I started crawling as fast as I could away from the sound until I
crawled head first into a wall myself. I stifled my cry of
pain so that the thing pursuing me wouldn't hear it and
started crawling along the wall hoping to find a door,
not a doorway which would corner me in a room, but
the front door so I could escape the house.

I kept crawling as fast as I could along the wall
passing two open doorways, which should have indicated to me that I had gone down the hallway and
past the bathroom and one bedroom, but I was so
concerned about the thing crawling after me that I
didn't pay attention to where I was in the house. I
made the u-turn at the end of the hallway and past the
second bedroom doorway headed back toward the
living room when I brushed up against something

going the other way. That meant that whatever was chasing me couldn't see in the dark either and had been following my crawling sound along the floor. Well, that made me shift into high gear and I started crawling faster than a black mamba on steroids! I felt something grab at my foot, but I was already in high gear and scooted away from whatever it was. I made the turn into the living room with whatever was chasing me along the wall sounding like it was closing the gap. I tried to crawl faster, but I thought my knees were going to come off and I felt like I was slowing down. Then just as I was about to give up and let whatever was behind me catch up and have me for lunch I came to the front door. I jumped to my feet, found the lock and fumbled it open, turned the door handle and opened the door to bright hot sunshine. I had been crawling so fast that I had actually worked up a sweat in the freezing house and had forgotten that it was actually cold in there. The brightness and heat together made me shift into an even higher gear since I was on my feet now and I started running as fast as I could toward my bicycle even though my knees still felt like they were going to fall off. When I was on my bicycle I took a quick glance back at the house to see if what had been chasing me had come outside to continue the chase. What I saw shocked me and turned me on at the same time, but I started pedaling and was away from there and several blocks away before I realized that I was shaking all over. What I had seen was Monica standing in the doorway STARK NAKED and motioning for me to come back. That picture was one that I conjured up in my mind on many occasions and you can guess what that did to me! Have I mentioned that she had ample breasts?

Chapter Twenty-three

Well, the morning was wasting away and all I had done was run into trouble again, not once mind you, but twice within minutes of each other! I wasn't sure right now if I could even mow a yard if I did find a safe one that needed mowing. And how would I know if it was safe to mow or not? I was beginning to think again that the reptilian alien things were taking over all the neighborhoods and that I was the only one who realized what was happening. *Couldn't any of the normal adults around here see that things weren't right? And why wouldn't my good buddy, Roger, not hang out with me much anymore? Did he tell his grandmother about the incident we shared and she told him not to hang around with me anymore if I was encouraging him to make up crazy stories like that? Did she think I was doing some kind of hallucinogenic drugs and was trying to get Roger to try them as well? **Or,** and this thought was almost too unbearable to im-*agine, *was she now one of them and had eaten Rog-er?*

All of these thoughts kept running through my little pea-sized brain as I kept pedaling along looking for a safe yard to mow. I was now on a street where I had mowed several yards that summer at least once and came to the first of those that certainly needed mow-ing again. Maybe the young couple that lived there had been waiting for me to come back because I didn't charge as much as professional yardmen and they couldn't afford to pay more or buy their own mower. I rode my bicycle into their driveway and went up to the door and knocked. The man of the house came to the door and seemed glad to see me. He said that they had been hoping that I would come back to mow their yard because I had done such a good job. He took out his wallet and paid me in advance and said that they would like for me to mow their yard on a regular basis if that was ok with me. I told him that I would check back weekly and mow it when it needed mowing. The agreement struck I got busy earning my three dollars. Everything went smoothly and I continued on to the next house on this street that I had mowed once before. Amazingly enough this yard needed mowing, too. After mowing that yard and stuffing another three bucks into my front pocket I pedaled on up the street to the next yard that I had previously mowed once.

The rest of the day went surprisingly well and I ended up mowing five yards that afternoon and making fourteen dollars. I even got back home on time and was resting on the sofa when my mom got home from work. At first she thought that I had probably wasted the whole day lounging around the house, but her attitude changed when I told her I had made fourteen dollars that day. She apologized for jumping to conclusions—not that I blamed her, given my track record—and told me to just take it easy while she fixed dinner.

Now, whether or not that was an intentional guilt trip I wasn't sure, but I jumped in anyway and helped with dinner. Fourteen dollars doesn't sound like much for a day's work today, but considering that my mom was only making the minimum wage of $1.15 per hour (it wouldn't go up to $1.25 until September of 1963) and an eight hour work day only brought in $9.20, her son making fourteen dollars in one day really did make her proud. And she actually did put in eight hour work days in 1963, starting work at 8:30 in the morning and not getting off until 5:00 in the afternoon with only thirty minutes for lunch. My dad netted about a hundred dollars per week at the service station after expenses which included paying the overhead, the Gordon's Potato Chip guy, the Phillips 66 people for gas and oil, the cigarette delivery man, the S&H Green Stamp people, and anyone else that he bought products from at wholesale to sell at retail in the service station.

When I went to the service station sometimes on weekends, especially Sundays, to help out I worked for free, considering it a privilege to work alongside the best mechanic ever. Besides, one or two scantily-clad hot babes might pull in for gas and I might just get a peek, if you know what I mean. Of course, with my luck, that didn't happen very often, but it did give me extra incentive to help out at the service station as often as possible. If I hadn't been mowing yards that summer I would have been at the service station a lot more, but the idea of having my own car when I turned sixteen tended to outweigh the idea of putting gas into the cars of hot babes. After all, when I got my own car I could pick up my own hot babes and drive around town like I was somebody. Was I ever in for a rude awakening during my later teenage years! Ninety-nine point nine percent of my time after I got a car was spent cruising around town looking for hot babes with my buddies in tow and, as you might expect, we didn't find any hot babes or cold babes or babes of any temperature in between. Just three shy, horny guys who ended up being three shy, horny, and lonely guys. Oh well, nobody ever said that life was fair for the average-looking, pimply-faced, shy, horny teenage boy who thought that playing jokes on girls (rather than being nice and helpful and chivalrous) would get them somewhere.

The rest of the evening went smoothly. We had chicken 'n dumplings, green beans cooked with a dab of bacon grease, fresh biscuits, and even banana pudding for desert. Those were all things that NOBODY made better than my mom! We all settled down in front of the television after dinner and Mom said to not even worry about the dishes, because I could do them in the morning after breakfast. Before long, we were all three snoozing in front of the television having stuffed ourselves, after a hard day's work.

Chapter Twenty-four

It was about five minutes after ten o'clock that night when all three of us were awakened by a loud rapping at the kitchen door. "Who in God's name could that be at this time of night?" my father asked, rather irritated.

"I don't know," my mom replied, "but it sounds urgent. You better see who it is."

My dad grudgingly got up from his easy chair, put on his house slippers and went to the door. The loud rapping hadn't stopped and I could tell that Dad was just about to tell somebody to "can it!" When Dad opened the door he was confronted by a somewhat frantic looking and babbling Mr. Kiches.

"It's Kelvin, it's Kelvin, he's missing! Is he over here?" Mr. Kiches frantically asked.

"We haven't seen Kelvin in days," my dad replied calmly, obviously trying to calm down Mr. Kiches.

"I know, I know," Mr. Kiches replied. "Kelvin's been missing for three days now and we're worried sick to death. Alma's been going on and on and crying for two days now and I just can't take no more of it!" exclaimed Mr. Kiches. Alma was Mrs. Kiches given name. "What're we going to do?" he asked my dad.

"Have you called the police?" Dad asked without talking down to Mr. Kiches like he was a scared little kid.

"Yes, yes, yes! They haven't been able to come up with any clues either, but I don't think they think this is a serious situation, being a poor kid and all. They think he probably just ran away and is hiding at a friend's house," Mr. Kiches was again sounding a bit frantic.

"Well, have you checked with all his friends, L.L.?" my dad asked. L.L. is how adults addressed Mr. Kiches, because those were the initials of his first and middle name. I never did know what they stood for and, quite frankly, because I wasn't too fond of Kelvin, I just didn't give a rat's patootey. And besides, if Kelvin never came back, it certainly wouldn't bother me. I would probably get Roger, if his grandmother hadn't eaten him, get some cigarettes, drag out the girlie magazine and have a little celebration party! I might even sneak us a little of the *Mogan David* wine that was supposed to be hidden at the back of one of the kitchen cupboards behind a stack of grocery store dishes. On special occasions and holidays I even got to have a little glass of it and Kelvin being gone forever would certainly qualify as a special occasion. But, once again, I digress and daydream. So back to the story.

"We've checked with all of Kelvin's friends that we know about except with your boy and Alma's been watchin' your house like a hawk watchin' a rabbit," Mr. Kiches explained.

By this time my mom and I were both standing next to my dad at the kitchen door listening intently to everything Mr. Kiches had to say. After all, we were both very concerned about the little fat butt wussy! Both very concerned that he would probably come back. Well, that last remark by Mr. Kiches about Mrs. Kiches watchin' our house like a hawk didn't set too well with Mom. "You tell that so-n-so you're married to that if she minded her own business she just might know where her little precious was!" my mom nearly yelled at him.

Dad gave her a look that said back off and let me handle this and Mom gave him a look that said "I will," but I'll tell you off later. And you can trust me when I say that she let him have it good just as soon as the door closed and Mr. Kiches was out of earshot.

"L.L., Bessie's right and you know it. If Alma kept a closer eye on that kid of yours and her nose out of other people's business you might know where Kelvin is right now. He's always trying to get my son in trouble and he was probably trying to get somebody else in trouble and got caught. He probably got turned over to the juvenile authorities. Have you checked there?"

"Well, I never," said Mr. Kiches and he turned around and stomped off. Looking back he said, "You'd think your neighbors would be a little more sympathetic than this!"

Which Dad followed with, "And you'd think your neighbors could mind their own business and raise their brat right!" Dad slammed the ، door shut and turned to face a rather ominous little woman who was getting ready to give him heck.

Well, while that little conversation went on for about thirty minutes, I went back to my bedroom and closed the door. Which is what I would have been asked to do anyway, but I didn't need to be told that more than a couple dozen times in situations like this before I caught on. With age comes wisdom, you know. I put my latest *Ricky Nelson* album, *Album Seven,* which came out the year before, on my portable record player and turned up the volume just enough to drown out the conversation going on in the kitchen. I crashed across the bed and started thinking about Kelvin being missing. I really did hope that he never came back, but I wondered if he was missing because the reptilian alien things had gotten him and eaten him. *If they had they wouldn't be hungry for a long time! Heck, they wouldn't have been able to eat all of him and probably had leftovers for a week stashed in a freezer somewhere. Maybe the Kiches should look in their big chest freezer in their storage shed! Might be some extra packages of fat in there!* At that thought I started to giggle and then settled back to listen to Ricky.

The next day I eagerly took off with the lawn mower as if I were going to look for more yards to mow. However, my plan was to do a little revisiting of a couple of places where I had nearly been captured by the reptilian alien things posing as Mrs. Root Beer Lady, the old man, or Monica. What I was hoping to find was some evidence that Kelvin had actually been abducted by the reptilian alien things and eaten. What kind of evidence would that be? I didn't know, but I would know it when I saw it.

I took the alleys and other back ways that I knew to get to those houses starting with Mrs. Root Beer Lady's house. My plan was to get as early a start as I could and sneak up to the back of the houses and try to peek in. I got to the house that I thought was the old hag's house and carefully looking around to make sure I wasn't being watched I snuck up to one of the back windows and peeked in. The curtains were pulled back and I had a full view of the kitchen where the old hag had tried to capture me. I didn't see anything out of the ordinary as I scanned around the room. I was just about to sneak around to a side window when the wide open jaws of the old hag or whatever it or she was with huge razor sharp teeth sprang up in the window right in front of me. The gaping jaws and I were only separated by a thin pane of glass and window screen. The huge mouth full of shark-like teeth snapped toward me and I must have jumped straight back ten feet falling on my butt, but the huge open mouth only bounced off the glass. Whatever it was sprang forward again snapping at me, but once again it bounced off the glass. I was sure that it was going to come crashing through the window and gulp me up like an alligator gulping down an unsuspecting duck swimming quietly on the water! As I sat there in the grass on my butt and leaning back on my hands it felt like I was thinking in slow motion and that the creature inside the house was moving in slow motion, too.

Gathering myself up I started running back the way I had come and turning the corner into the back alley I ran smack dab into the arms of Monica, my face slamming into those ample breasts that I think I have mentioned before. I nearly knocked her down, but she grabbed hold of me and steadied us both looking into my eyes with both horror and pleasant surprise at the same time. She held me tight at arm length and looked me up and down and said, "What's wrong, little Jimmy? Why are you in such a hurry?"

"I was just at that house over there and there's a monster inside that's trying to get out and eat me!" I exclaimed.

"Now, Jimmy, there's no such thing as monsters and you're much too old to believe in them if there were," she cooed in that soft soothing voice that I remembered from our first meeting.

Older and wiser. That's what ran at lightening speed through my head and I jerked loose from her grasp and ran off down the alley toward where I had left my bicycle as fast as my clod hoppers would go! *I was too old to believe in monsters if there were monsters!* That was a clue that I got immediately! *Older and wiser* I thought as I ran. I got to my bicycle, jumped on and started pedaling back toward home. Enough of this nonsense! Some might say that it was a coincidence that I happened to run into Monica while fleeing from some hallucination that I was having probably brought on by having smoked too many cigarettes, drunk too much wine and coffee, and looked at a girlie magazine a few times too many. Well, that was what I would have called a bunch of psychological bull poopy if I had known what psychological really meant. Someone, somewhere, someday would believe what had been happening to me that summer. All I wanted to do was mow yards to earn money to buy a car in a couple of years, even a 1959 Studebaker. Someone, somewhere, someday!

Chapter Twenty-Five

All of a sudden, as I was pedaling harder than ever back toward home, I remembered why I was out sneaking around in the first place. I wanted to find evidence that Kelvin had been abducted and hopefully eaten by the reptilian alien things. I slowed down and decided to turn around and head off toward Monica's house, because she was obviously not home and that would mean being safe while I snooped around. When I got within about a block of Monica's house, or, again, what I thought was Monica's house, I parked by bicycle and mower in a safe place and headed for the house that I honestly believed to be where the gorgeous blond lived.

When I came up behind her house I again looked around to make sure no one was watching me and then snuck up to one of the back windows. Most of the houses around here were of the same cookie cutter type and so I decided that kitchens might not be where clues to Kelvin's disappearance would be, but rather they would be in a bedroom or bathroom. The reptilian alien thing that had taken on Monica's appearance probably lured old Kelvin into her bedroom where she proceeded to change back into the reptilian alien thing and started eating on him. Since he was so fat she probably called others of her kind over to help her feast on Kelvin. So it had to be in her bedroom that I would see some remnant of Kelvin.

So I snuck up to the first bedroom window and peeked in. As with the old hag's house, the curtains were open and I had a clear view into the bedroom. I looked around the room, but I didn't see anything that looked like "evidence" of a crime scene and silently cursed to myself that that appeared to be the case.

Remember, if Kelvin were gone for good, Roger and I would be very happy campers! That is, if Roger were still alive. Ok, there was one other bedroom so I snuck around to that one and peeked in. Again, the curtains were open and I had a clear view of the entire room. As hard as I tried and as much as I wanted to find some left over evidence of Kelvin, there just wasn't anything laying around anywhere in the room.

But wait, was that something under the back corner of the pink, frilly-lace covered bed closest to the window that I was looking through? Was it just a house slipper or a pair of panties? Remember, I was just a horny fourteen-year old boy and hallucinating that what I saw was a pair of panties was pretty normal.

I had to get inside and find out for sure that it wasn't a leftover piece of Kelvin. I pulled at the bottom of the screen and it wasn't hooked. It pulled up easily and so I tried pulling up on the bottom of the double hung window. It slid up like it had been greased with lard and I had to actually grab at it to keep it from slamming up into the top of the window frame. I leaned over and looked just inside the window to see if it was safe to crawl in and saw that the bottom of the window wasn't too far from the floor. I crawled through and onto to floor and then crawled carefully over to what I had seen under the end of the bed. When I got close enough I reached up and turned on the bedside lamp and then looked under the bed. What I saw both scared me and pleased me all at the same time. It was a man's sneaker and it appeared to be covered with red paint. *No, not red paint, it HAD to be BLOOD! IT HAD TO BE KELVIN'S SNEAKER AND KELVIN'S BLOOD! IT JUST HAD TO BE! PLEASE LET IT BE KELVIN'S SNEAKER AND BLOOD!* When kids hate other kids as much as I hated Kelvin they can wish for some pretty terrible things. I had never really paid much attention to Kelvin's wardrobe, but it certainly looked big enough to be Kelvin's. I looked around to see if there was anything I could put the sneaker into so that I could carry it back and show the police. I would lie and say that I found it in the alley behind the house while I was out looking for yards to mow. That way they wouldn't know that I had entered the house illegally, unless, of course, they dusted for fingerprints. There wasn't anything that I could put the sneaker in so I just reached over and picked it up and started crawling back toward the window. So far, so good. The window was still up and the screen still unfastened so I climbed out and into the backyard. I still didn't see anyone around so I thought I was in the clear, but just then a voice yelled at me, "What do you think you're doing, punk?"

I looked toward the house from where the voice seemed to be coming and there was a man in a t-shirt and a pair of boxer shorts standing with his hands on his hips and staring intently at me. My first thought was to run away, because I didn't think he would be able to catch me considering the size of his beer gut and the fact that he was only dressed in his underwear.

"I asked you a question, boy," he yelled at me.

"None of your dang business," I yelled back and started walking away in the opposite direction of where I had left my bicycle and mower. *Had I actually talked that way to an adult?* Boy, I hope my parents never found out about that. That would be worse than them finding out that I had snuck into a stranger's house to snoop around!

"Get yer skinny butt back here, punk," the man yelled and when I looked back he was trotting toward me, because trotting was all he was capable of doing. I shifted into a sprint and circled around to the front of Monica's house, across her lawn and the lawn of the man chasing me and down the other side of his house. By the time he had gotten to the front of Monica's house I was sprinting down the alley and back to my bicycle. I quickly tied the sneaker to the back of my bicycle with the shoelace, jumped on and headed on my way. I was well out of sight by the time the man got to his front yard. I figured that the sneaker was enough evidence to get at least one adult to believe my incredible story about reptilian alien things that were feasting on teenage boys. Yeh, right! That was going to happen. But, maybe this was Kelvin's sneaker and maybe it would get the police on the trail of the killer or killers and once they saw what they were up against I would be hailed as a hero for warning the world about these creatures. *Yeh, that's what would happen. I would be a big hero!*

Chapter Twenty-Six

There was still one house that I had originally planned to investigate, but that was before I had found the sneaker. Now that I had this evidence I was sure there was no need to investigate any other houses. I figured at that particular moment that this one blood-stained sneaker would be all the police would need to shift their investigation into high gear! So, I pedaled on back home to put the sneaker in a bag and hide it in the shed until I could tell my dad what I suspected. Then Dad would call the police and give them the sneaker so they could investigate whatever kind of horrible crime had taken place in Monica's bedroom.

When Dad got home and dinner was over I asked him to come out to the shed and I told him my story and showed him the sneaker. Now, one thing that I hadn't thought about is that adults don't tend to think like teenagers. Dad's first response was, "Are you the stupidest dang kid that ever lived? Have I not taught you anything about life? What if this confounded sneaker is from a crime? If I call the police and give it to them then WE'RE involved and the person who committed the crime might come after us! How dang stupid can one kid be? You're going to take this sneaker back to where you found it and make sure no one sees you putting it back. Is that clear, son?"

Well, put yourself in my fourteen year old shoes (not that my shoes were fourteen years old, they were only about eight month old Keds – you see, my feet were still growing and I had to get new shoes at least once a year). What would you have told my dad after that little tirade? Probably not what I said next, "But, Dad, this looks just like the sneakers that Kelvin wears and it must be about the size he wears, I mean look at how big he is, or was. If we don't report this Kelvin might never be found or his poor parents might never know what happened to him."

That last little bit of psychological poo poo was what got him. "You're right, son," he replied, "I would want to know what happened to you if you disappeared. I'll tell you what we're going to do. First, we're going to ask the Kiches if this is Kelvin's sneaker and if it is, then we'll go to the police with it and you'll tell them where you found it. You'll probably have to take them to the place where you found it."

I had to agree with this bit of strategy on my dad's part, but then I realized that if I had to go back to Monica's house, even the alley behind it where I told dad I found the sneaker, the man next door was sure to come out and tell the police the truth. Maybe someday I would learn to plan out my stories better before I told them, especially when I told them to my parents. I was pretty sure that Dad believed that I had found the sneaker while I was out looking for yards to mow and that I was so upset that I came straight home instead of looking for more yards to mow. But if I had to go back to the alley behind Monica's house I was going to be in deeper do do than I had ever been in, because the guy next door would no doubt tell them that I had broken into Monica's house.

"Come on," Dad said. "Let's go over to the Kiches and show them the sneaker. This isn't going to be easy if this is Kelvin's sneaker. You might prepare yourself for Mrs. Kiches to break down and start crying, or worse." We walked over to the Kiches' front door and rang the doorbell, which sounded like the bells down at the Catholic church on Sunday (we had driven by there a few times when they were ringing). My parents weren't church-goers and didn't press me to attend church either. I had been baptized in a Baptist church when I was twelve, primarily because I had heard somewhere (probably from Roger's grandmother) that when children turned twelve their parents were no longer responsible for their sins. However, I had quit going about a year ago because I was getting nowhere trying to gain the attentions of the minister's daughter, Maude.

The door was answered by Mr. Kiches and he gave Dad a very stern "what the devil are you doing at my front door" look. Since he didn't say anything, Dad began telling him my story. Mr. Kiches then stared at me with a similar angry look and then turned his attention back to Dad. Dad opened the paper bag and held it out for Mr. Kiches to look in and tell us if the shoe was Kelvin's or not. It was at that moment that Mrs. Kiches walked up and wanted to know what was going on and what did we want? Mr. Kiches hadn't had time to look into the bag, but backed up a step and related Dad's story to her. Not being terribly shy, Mrs. Kiches stepped forward and grabbed the bag and dumped it on the floor just inside the front door where there was plenty of light to see the sneaker. She had actually started to tear up a little, but when the sneaker with the red stain came to a rest at her feet the tears dried up fast and she looked at Mr. Kiches with a look that would have made me run for the hills (if there had been any hills to run to in central Florida)! Something BIG was about to happen and Dad and I both knew it as we glanced at each other.

The look that Mrs. Kiches was giving her husband was one of those that would make anyone take a couple of steps backward and that was exactly what dad and I did. Without taking her "I'm going to kill you" gaze from Mr. Kiches, she said to us, "This isn't Kelvin's sneaker, it's his sneaker (referring to Mr. Kiches) and that isn't blood, it's red paint he spilled on it while painting the bench on the back patio. Where did you say you found it?" she asked me without taking her glaring stare from Mr. Kiches.

"Tell her where you found the sneaker, son," Dad instructed me, "and tell the truth."

"I found it in the alley behind a house where I had mowed the yard a couple of times. I had gone back to mow the yard again when I saw it. I thought it looked like the ones Kelvin wears." (I carefully kept it out of the past tense.)

"Who lives in that house?" Mrs. Kiches asked me, again not looking at me, but continuing to stare intently at her husband.

I looked up at my dad who was watching me carefully to see if he could figure out if I was telling the truth. Parents are good at that you know. "Tell her, son," he once again instructed me.

"All I know is that she calls herself Monica," I offered. I didn't see any sense in getting into the feelings I had had about her or that she was really a reptilian alien thing in disguise.

"And is this woman named Monica a blonde?" Mrs. Kiches asked me.

Well, I figured I was caught now, so I might as well tell the truth. I was obviously going to be found out right here and now standing in the dark just outside the living room of Kelvin's house. What kind of irony would that be? Kelvin, if alive, was going to get me good this time and he hadn't even tried.

"Well, son?" my dad both asked and instructed.

"Blonde," was all I offered at this particular moment.

Mr. Kiches hadn't moved even one muscle during this minor inquisition, which I thought was directed at me.

"YOU SORRY, CHEATING PIG!" Mrs. Kiches yelled at her husband. That took him back a couple of steps, but Mrs. Kiches moved three steps toward him for his two back. "YOU SORRY PIECE OF CRAP! YOU'VE BEEN WITH THAT BLOND HARLOT AGAIN, HAVEN'T YOU?" She was still yelling, just in case you don't understand why I put that in capital letters.

Chapter Twenty-seven

Dad's eyes were almost as wide as mine as we both backed up a few more steps before turning and heading back for our house. As we walked slowly back to our house, so we could hear what Mrs. Kiches was yelling at Mr. Kiches, she kept yelling at him with the door standing wide open for all the neighborhood to hear. "MY BABY'S MISSING AND YOU'RE OUT DOING IT WITH THAT BLOND HARLOT AGAIN! YOU PROMISED YOU WERE THROUGH WITH YOUR PHILANDERING!" I didn't know what "philandering" meant, but I had an idea that it had to do with Mr. Kiches appreciation, like mine, of that knock-dead gorgeous blond with the ample breasts. Mrs. Kiches started in on her husband again, DON'T YOU CARE THAT MY BABY'S STILL MISSING? WELL, YOU KNOW WHERE YOU'RE GOING TO SLEEP TO-NIGHT, MISTER! JUST WAIT UNTIL I GET MY HANDS ON THAT BLOND HARLOT OF YOURS!"

Dear God, please don't make me go with her to show her where Monica lives. It wasn't so much that I was afraid of being with Mrs. Kiches, but, remember, the man next door would tell that I had broken into the house. Dad ushered me into the house and related the whole scenario to Mom. I thought she might have gotten angry at me, but she just smiled bigger and bigger as dad told her what had happened at the Kiches, until she started laughing so hard that tears welled up in her eyes. Her laughing was very contagious and within seconds Dad and I were laughing just as hard.

I don't know what went on the rest of the night over at the Kiches' house, but Mrs. Kiches could be heard yelling for several more hours. I didn't sleep very much that night figuring that the next morning I would have to show Mrs. Kiches where that "BLOND HARLOT" lived so she could do whatever it was to her that she had in mind. Of course, I knew that Monica probably wouldn't be there because these reptilian alien things seemed to know what was coming before it ever happened. That and the man next door would probably come out and reveal the horrible truth about me breaking into the house to steal whatever it was that I had stolen. *But, on the other hand, if Monica was there the ensuing fight might be worth seeing.* Just another one of those mind consuming adult problems that a fourteen-year-old boy had to deal with.

As it turned out, we didn't hear anymore from the Kiches' for nearly a week. We went about our normal activities around my house including my going out to mow yards. It actually turned out to be a fairly normal few days. I mowed yards, Mom went to work, Dad went to work, and I didn't have any encounters with monsters of any kind. I was just starting to think that I had been imagining everything when one day, while I was getting ready to untie my mower from my bicycle and start mowing a new yard in a neighborhood far removed from Monica's, I felt a light tap on my shoulder. Even though I thought I had calmed down concerning the events of the summer, I jumped about two feet when I felt the tap on my shoulder. Spinning around quickly and ready to impale whatever had tapped me on the shoulder with my grass clippers I was face to face with Mr. Kiches.

"I just wanted to let you know that we're watching you, sonny boy!" he literally growled at me (and that should have been a clue to run for those proverbial hills again!).

"What do you want?" I asked trying to sound brave. "Why did you follow me? I didn't know that sneaker was yours. I was just trying to help you and Mrs. Kiches find Kelvin," I lied.

"What we want is for you to keep your snoopy little butt out of our business," he said in that growling tone. "And it's none of your business why we follow you. Just know that we are always watching and are closer than you might think."

"What do you mean by 'we'?" I foolishly asked, but I had to know if what I was thinking was true.

"As your kind would say, you know darn good and well who we are," he said as he moved his face a little closer to mine.

As he got closer I immediately recognized that horrible breath I smelled every time one of the reptilian alien things tried to eat me. That made me back quickly up several steps and get ready to run, even if it meant leaving my bicycle and mower behind. But right at that moment, the screen door of the house where I was getting ready to mow the yard slammed open hard against the front of the house and Mr. Teables, the man who lived there, came rushing out and down the stairs toward us.

"You get away from that kid, mister!" he yelled as he was approaching us. "You lay one finger on him and I'll crush your head like a grape in a wine press!" Now Mr. Teables wasn't the kind of guy you wanted to mess with. He was probably around six-foot six inches tall and probably weighed in at around 250 pounds, none of which was fat. But Mr. Teables didn't know what he was dealing with here. These creatures from another world in a galaxy far away could change back to their reptilian appearance and swallow him up whole in one gulp!

"No problem, man," Mr. Kiches said in his normal human voice as he was backing away from me. "The kid is my next door neighbor and I saw him as I was driving by and just wanted to say hello."

Feeling much braver now that Mr. Teables was next to me I looked up at him and said, "He's lying! He was threatening to hurt me because he thinks I know where his son disappeared to. But I don't. I think he killed him and disposed of the body somewhere where no one could ever find it." I didn't want to really sound bizarre and tell Mr. Teables that I thought Mr. Kiches had also eaten his son.

"Why you little brat," Mr. Kiches said and moved toward me in a threatening manner again. Mr. Teables stepped between Mr. Kiches and me and gave him a little shove that sent Mr. Kiches reeling backward and hard onto his butt. "I told you to leave the boy alone and I'm not going to tell you again."

For a split second I know that I saw Mr. Kiches skin start to turn scaly looking, but it quickly stopped as Mr. Teables hovered over him. Mr. Kiches scrambled to his feet and started moving away from us as he said, "I'll deal with the both of you later."

"I'll be waiting," Mr. Teables responded. "Now get the devil out of here and don't ever come around here again!"

Mr. Kiches, or whatever he or it was, scurried back to his car, which was parked about a half a block away and sped off down the street.

"Thanks, Mr. Teables," I said. "He really was threatening me."

"That's what I thought when I looked out the window," he replied. "If he ever bothers you again you just let me know where he lives and I beat the holy crap out of him. Ok?"

"Yes sir," I answered. "I'll get busy on the yard now."

Chapter Twenty-eight

As I was mowing Mr. Teables' yard I thought about what had just happened with Mr. Kiches and that he never did say what he meant by 'we'. Of course, I had my suspicions that Mr. Kiches, and maybe Mrs. Kiches, were reptilian alien things. Actually, I had a harder time believing that Mrs. Kiches was one, because she was even more evil and hateful than the monsters that had been stalking me lately. Then it occurred to me why we hadn't seen the Kiches for several days: Mr. Kiches had not only killed and eaten Kelvin, but he must have also done away with the woman who thought that he was her husband. That also meant that the reptilian alien thing that was now posing as Mr. Kiches had killed and eaten the real Mr. Kiches! Was it possible that my family was also in danger from the thing that now posed as Mr. Kiches? Maybe he or it hadn't bothered us because we were living too close to it and it would be too obvious if something did happen to us. Could it be that the thing that we knew as Mr. Kiches was also the old man in the group of three that I had had contact with during the past few weeks of my summer vacation? Some vacation! I had to mow yards to earn money and had been pursued by reptilian alien things all summer. If this was a summer vacation then I wanted to go to school twelve months a year.

I continued mowing and kept thinking about lots of things, not just what had happened to me that summer. I had been so preoccupied with what was happening to me and the fact that I had to work so hard to earn money to buy a car when I turned sixteen that I had neglected a couple of other important people in my life. Looking back on it now I know that my neglect of Leasure, my girlfriend you will remember me mentioning a while back, was probably what made her drop me as we progressed into the tenth grade. And then there was Roger, my best buddy of all time. I had drug him into my little nightmare and he had now been essentially banned from having anything to do with me, although he did sneak around once in a while to share a cigarette and look at the now ragged girlie magazine. He wasn't angry with me for including him (he was glad that he had gone with me that day, probably more because of meeting Monica than anything else), but his grandmother now thought that I was some kind of drug-taking beatnik and she wasn't going to let me influence her little grandson in the wrong way.

Leasure and I had been going steady for almost three years and even though we had never done anything more sexual in nature than hold hands and kiss a few times when our parents weren't watching, I think we really did like each other a lot. If I hadn't been so neglectful that summer we might have been high school sweethearts for the next three years. As it turned out during my entire three-year high school life I didn't go steady with anyone. Not that I didn't have a few opportunities, but I think my experiences during the summer of my fourteenth year had a lot to do with me becoming more shy and almost reclusive. I had been turned into someone who didn't trust anyone, which led to not having many friends and me becoming somewhat antisocial. I probably could have revived my fifth and sixth grade romance with Tessia or responded positively to Shondra's advances in the eleventh grade or in the twelfth grade I could have had my way with the school nymph, Lisa, when she showed interest in me or accepted Eva's invitation to take her to the senior prom, because her boyfriend was away serving in the Army (he had graduated the year before) but then there was Harmony. But even though I wanted a girlfriend more than any other guy in high school, with the exception of the school homosexual, Brulee, I was just too shy and suspicious of everyone, including any hot girl that might have had an interest in me.

My friendship with Roger essentially ended when we moved away from the old neighborhood, but I heard that his grandmother died shortly thereafter and he had to move back in with his mom permanently. A few weeks later I heard that she took Roger and moved to the northwest somewhere with one of her boyfriends who was a truck driver. Roger had been a good friend and we had shared lots of good childhood experiences together, from learning about women by looking at the girlie magazine every time we got a chance to sharing cigarettes and wine every chance we got. Just two guys who wanted to experience the world they were growing up in during the late 1950s and early 1960s. Roger and I had been buddies for about eight years and it all went down the tubes when we moved away.

I finished mowing Mr. Teables' yard, got paid, and cautiously moved on to my next yard, constantly looking around for any sign of Mr. Kiches or one of the other reptilian alien things. I kept thinking to myself that this whole summer was just one of those short dreams where even years could pass quickly in about ten seconds. But it seemed too real to be a dream and if it was a dream, shouldn't I wake up soon? I mowed three more yards that day without incident and headed back home so that I would be there when my mom got home from work.

The first thing I noticed when I rode my bicycle into our driveway was the eerie silence that seemed to encompass the Kiches' house. It almost seemed to be darker over there even though it was a sunny day. The Rambler station wagon was gone and all of the curtains were closed. Out of curiosity, I walked over to their driveway to get a closer look after I had put my bicycle and the lawn mower away. I hadn't taken more than two steps onto their property when it felt like the temperature, which was in the high eighties that day, instantly dropped about thirty degrees. I literally shivered and decided that it wouldn't be wise to proceed in my investigation. I turned around and headed back into our yard and sat down on the kitchen steps. That was just too strange to be more than anything but a dream, but I still wasn't waking up. I even pinched myself hard to see if that would wake me up. Since it really hurt I figured I was wide awake. The simple solution here was to stay away from the Kiches property and maybe, just maybe, they would leave me alone. As it turned out, their leaving me alone wouldn't be a problem.

Chapter Twenty-nine

As usual, Dad was up first the next morning and was sitting at the dining room table sipping on a cup of coffee and smoking his first Camel cigarette of the day when he heard a commotion going on outside. He got up and peeked out the kitchen window to discover five or six police cars pulled up out front of the Kiches' house. There were at least eight uniformed and two plainclothes officers "prowling" around the Kiches' house. Dad woke up both Mom and me and told us to get dressed and to come into the kitchen, because he had something to show us. When we walked into the kitchen he told us to look out the kitchen window. We did as directed and then turned around wide-eyed asking Dad what was going on next door. He didn't know yet, but he was going out to see if he could find out.

Dad was gone only a few minutes when he came back into the house to inform us that the police had said to not go onto the Kiches' property again because they were conducting an investigation into the disappearance of all three of the Kiches. Dad reiterated the police instructions to me in particular and said that he didn't want to come home that night to find out that I had been arrested for trespassing. I assured him that I didn't want anything to do with the cops and he gave me a funny look when I said that.

"You're not in some kind of trouble, are you?" he asked me.

"NO SIR!" I exclaimed.

"You sound a little too definite if you ask me. I better not find out that you know something that you aren't telling us," he said.

I knew exactly what he meant by that and that I wasn't too old to get a whipping and be grounded until

I was fifty. All I could hope for at this point was that the police wouldn't connect me in any way to the mysterious disappearance of the Kiches. However, I had already decided that I was going to keep a close watch on as much of the police activity around the Kiches' house that day as I could get away with. Mom and Dad headed off to work as usual without the police paying any attention to them, so I figured they wouldn't even notice me even if I was sitting outside on the doorstep.

Going outside to sit on the doorstep and watch their activity was one more mistake on my part. As Dad would have said to me for about the ten thousandth time, "That's what you get for thinking." I hadn't been sitting out on the steps for more than thirty minutes when one of the plainclothes officers walked over to me.

"What's your name, kid?" he asked in his best cop voice.

"James," I answered.

"Do you have any brothers or sisters?" he asked.

"No sir," I replied.

"Are the two adults who left earlier your parents?" he continued with his questions.

"Yes sir," I replied not offering any more information than I had to.

"You're just a fountain of information, aren't you?" he said, as if reading my mind.

"I'm just trying to answer the questions you're asking me, sir," I said.

"How old are you, James?" he continued.

"Fourteen," I replied sounding almost proud that I had made it that far.

"Oh, really! You telling the truth, boy? You certainly don't look fourteen," he stated matter-of-factly.

I thought that my response was pretty adult, but as soon as I said it I knew that it was about as stupid a thing to say to a cop as a teenage kid could come up with. "Well then," I replied, "you must not be much of a detective."

"You better watch your smart mouth, mister, or I'll be running you downtown to take a lie detector test."

"Yes sir. I'm sorry," I lied, but sounded properly remorseful.

"I'm going to ask you some important questions now and you better answer truthfully," he directed me. "If I think you're not telling the truth I'll run you in. Is that clear?"

"Yes sir," I told him knowing full well that I would lie when it was necessary to keep me out of trouble.

"Good," he said. "Now, the first question. When was the last time you saw any of the Kiches?"

I knew I had to tell the cop about what had happened a couple of days ago when dad and I had gone over to the Kiches with the sneaker. "Night before last," I said. "Dad and I were talking to Mr. And Mrs. Kiches at their front door."

"Their front door?" he questioned. "The door at the front of their house?"

Yes, you dumb butt so-called investigator, I thought to myself, but replied, "That's the one."

He gave me that "don't get smart with me" look again, but went on to his next question, which wasn't what I would have thought he would ask, but then I'm not a well-educated, smart police investigator. "Did Mr. And Mrs. Kiches say if they were going anywhere when you and your dad were talking to them?"

"No sir," I said matter-of-factly.

"Yep, just an overflowing fountain of information," he said sounding a little less than serious. "Was their car here this morning when you and your parents got up?"

"The first thing my dad noticed over there this morning was all of you guys prowling around," I explained. "So I don't think their car was there this morning."

"Well, now maybe we're getting somewhere," he said meaning that I had offered more information than asked for. "Was their car here yesterday or last night?" "I was out mowing yards yesterday and when I got home around four o'clock it wasn't there," I said. "I don't know if they came home later, because I didn't look out after my mom got home around five o'clock. Dad got home around 6:30 and he didn't say anything about it. We sat down to dinner right after Dad got home. Mom and I had been busy fixing dinner after she got home so we didn't even think about checking on the neighbors. So, I guess they could have come home last night and then left really early this morning."

"Glory be, boy!" he exclaimed. "Get you started and you won't shut up."

"I'm just trying to be more helpful like you wanted," I replied with obvious irritation in my voice. "Make up your mind what you want!"

"Ok, sorry," he said actually sounding apologetic. "I asked and you answered like a real pro. So, you're saying that your parents probably won't be home before around five or six o'clock tonight? Do you think they would be willing to talk to us before you have dinner?"

"I'm pretty sure that would be ok if that's what you want," I answered.

"I'll come back tonight around six o'clock," he said. "Can you let your parents know that I'm coming back before they get home?"

"Yes sir, I'll do that as soon as we get done here," I replied.

"We're done here," he said and turned to walk away. "Oh, thank you, James, for your cooperation."

"Anything to help out," I lied again. When he had gone back over into the Kiches' yard I went inside and called Mom first and then Dad to let them know what had gone on and that the investigator was coming back that night to question them. They wanted to know if the policeman had indicated what was going on and

I told them no. Dad figured we would find out that night when the policeman came back to question them. What we would find out that night was pretty shocking to my parents, but I wasn't in the least surprised even though I acted horrified.

Chapter Thirty

Promptly at six o'clock there was a knock at the kitchen door and Dad got up from the dining room table where he had been sitting enjoying yet another cigarette. He peeked out first and then opened the door to the plainclothes cop standing in the carport. The cop flashed his identification, identified himself as Sergeant Morgan, and Dad invited him inside. Dad asked if he had had dinner and the cop replied that he had grabbed a quick bite out on Memorial Boulevard at the privately-run burger joint. That "burger joint" was just across the side street next to my dad's service station and I knew it well. I often went over there to get Dad and me lunch when I was helping out at the station. Besides, the daughter of the couple who ran the "burger joint" was a knockout and always around after school and on weekends helping out. She was my age, but of course she wasn't interested in me no matter how much I tried to talk to her.

Dad invited the cop to have a seat at the table not wanting him to get too deep into the house by inviting him into the living room. It was just Dad's way with strangers. They were welcome, but not too welcome. The cop took a seat at the table and opened his notebook, which looked to be full of notes already.

"What can we help you with?" dad asked.

"Well, it seems that not only have your neighbors disappeared, it appears that there was foul play over there in that house," the cop said.

"Foul play," dad repeated. "What do you mean by that?"

"There was blood all over the place in their kitchen and living room, but we didn't find anything that might be considered a murder weapon," the cop informed my dad. Then looking over at me and then back at my dad he said, "Do you think it's wise for the kid to be hearing this kind of stuff?"

"The kid, as you refer to him, is growing up fast and it won't hurt him to know that bad things happen in this world, sometimes even close to home," Dad informed the cop.

"Whatever you say, sir," Sergeant Morgan said sounding a little incredulous. "I just have a few questions for you and your wife and then I'll be out of here and you can get to your dinner."

"My wife doesn't have anything different to say than me, so you can ask me all your questions and I'll answer for both of us," dad informed him.

"Well, that's a little out of the ordinary, sir, but we'll go with it for now," the cop said. "My first question for you is when did you last see the Kiches' or their car?"

"It's been a couple of days since we saw them," Dad replied.

"When you and your boy were talking to them at their front door?" the cop asked.

"That's right," Dad answered.

"Didn't it seem strange to you that you didn't see them or their car the past couple of days?" the cop asked.

"We aren't the closest of friends," Dad said. "We don't ask where they go or where they've been and they don't ask us, but Alma, Mrs. Kiches, is about as nosy as any woman ever has been."

"Did it ever bother you that she was sticking her nose in your business?" the Sergeant asked.

"Naw," Dad said. "Some women are just nosier than others, but they're all that way to some degree. So, what do you think happened over there?"

"Well, sir, it looks like someone got hurt pretty bad or maybe even killed," the Sergeant answered. "There was a lot of blood for that not to be the case. We've cordoned off the property and you folks shouldn't be nosing around over there while our investigation is ongoing and that might be for several days."

"You don't have to worry about us nosing around anywhere," Dad said, sounding somewhat irritated by the implication.

"Well, unless you've got something to add to the investigation I'll be going so you can have your dinner," the cop said.

"We'll be the first to let you know," Dad told him. "And don't worry, Sergeant, we won't be leaving town either." Although it sounded funny to me, there wasn't any humor in Dad's expression.

"Funny," said Sergeant Morgan as he opened the kitchen door to leave. "Thanks for your help."

The door closed and Dad looked over at me with that "you better not be holding anything back look."

"Go get your mom and let's get some dinner on the table," he instructed. I did as I was told and Mom and I got dinner fixed in no time. As usual, Dad sat at the dinner table and smoked another cigarette while dinner was being prepared. He told Mom what had transpired and what the cop suspected had happened next door while she was out of the room. Mom asked if the cop had said anything about checking the hospital to see if one of the Kiches had been admitted recently. Dad said that would have showed some smarts on the cops' part and he didn't think they were all that clever, especially Sergeant Morgan.

That was all that was said about the cop or the Kiches the rest of the evening as we finished dinner and settled in for some television. There was little that kept Dad and me away from the television set after dinner, not even the disappearance of irritable neighbors.

Chapter Thirty-one

Although the Kiches' property was "cordoned off," not one cop showed up the next day to continue the investigation into the Kiches' disappearance. Dad instructed me to stay home from mowing yards for a few days and keep an eye on the cops when they came back around. His main concern was that they would snoop around our house while no one was home. Dad had a high respect for the police, but was more than a little irritated and concerned about Sergeant Morgan. To say that he didn't trust this one cop was an understatement.

I hung out in the carport, driveway, backyard, and road my bicycle up and down the street, but never more than four or five houses away. As suspicious as dad was I figured that the cops were undercover somewhere close by and might come snooping around if they thought I was leaving the house for a while. However, that didn't happen on that day. Strangely enough, I didn't see anyone on our street that day. That was actually pretty unusual since at least one adult in every family that I knew on our street had to go to work every day. My parents were always the first to leave every morning for work and I often sat around, especially during the summer, watching one after the other up and down the street leaving for work. This morning, however, I didn't see one adult on the street leave for work. My parents had left at their regular time, so it was hard to believe that everyone else had left earlier than them. I thought about knocking on a few doors, but after what had happened at Mrs. Chyspo's, I wasn't too eager to go looking for more trouble.

I got tired of just pedaling my bicycle up down the same street and returned to the house and parked in the carport. I sat down on the steps and just stared at the house next door trying to imagine, although it was scaring me, what had happened to the neighbors – not that I missed them or wished for them to miraculously return. I imagined the reptilian alien things, which I suspected the Kiches to be associated with or even actually be themselves, either turning on them and gobbling them up or them having invited all the other neighbors to their house where they killed and feasted on them all night, thus all the blood in the house. I would have liked to tell the cops my theory, but then that would have made me look a little ridiculous not only to them but to my parents as well. And I certainly didn't need to look any more ridiculous to them than I already had.

As I said, no cops showed up that day at the crime scene and no one seemed to be going to work, but for the first time in about two weeks Roger emerged from his house and came over to join me on the steps.

"So, where have you been hiding the past couple of weeks?" I inquired of my very best buddy of all time.

"I haven't been hiding!" he exclaimed. "I'm no yellow-bellied chicken even if you think I am."

"Sorry," I said, "I didn't mean to say that you were. But when we have spent almost every waking minute hanging out together the past few years I started wondering what was up."

"My grandmother has kept me under lock and key," he told me. "She didn't want me hanging out with you or having anything to do with the mysterious things that seem to be happening around this neighborhood lately."

"Come to think of it, I haven't seen your grandmother out and about either," I responded, "and she's always going out to the store for something."

"Well, she's just as scared as everyone else on this street and she has everything that we need to survive for two or three years," Roger informed me.

"What do you mean, "just as scared as everyone else on this street"? I asked him, wondering if there had been some sort of meeting among the neighbors except my family.

"She's been talking to the other people on the street and everyone is wondering what is going on around here," he informed me. "The other people who live around here think weird things are going on."

"What kind of weird things?" I asked.

"Well, after Granny told other people what I told her you and me had experienced at that blond woman's house, they thought it was pretty weird," he said like it was nothing to blab everything to granny.

"Oh, great!" I exclaimed. "Now everyone on the street thinks I'm some kind of weirdo because you can't keep your fat trap shut!"

"I was in shock that day when I got home," he explained, "and Granny wouldn't stop asking questions and badgering me until I told her what had happened. Besides, she didn't believe it. She just thought you were on some kind of drugs or something."

"And now she's told the whole neighborhood that I'm some drug crazed weirdo!" I said rather loudly. "No wonder no one will let me mow their yard in this neighborhood. My dad's been wondering about that and I didn't have any explanation, which didn't make him too happy."

"I'm sorry, man," Roger apologized, and I knew by his tone that he meant it. "You're my best friend and I'd never do anything to change that. Granny just kept on and on at me and I couldn't take it anymore. You would have done the same thing in my place."

"Yeh, probably so," I said more calmly. "But that still doesn't change everybody's image of me."

"I know," he said sounding even more apologetic. "If I could do anything about it I would."

"You could tell everybody the truth, but then they'd probably hate you, too," I said. "Don't worry about it. Maybe it will blow over in a few weeks. Besides, the Kiches' disappearance should keep their minds off me for a while."

"THE KICHES DISAPPEARED!" he yelled. "OH, CRAP! GRANNY DOESN'T KNOW THAT!"

"Keep it down, man," I almost whispered. "The cops were here yesterday snooping around and told my dad that they suspected foul play over there. Maybe even murder!"

"MURDER?" he yelled out.

"Quiet, dude," I again almost whispered.

"Sorry," Roger said. "Things are getting really weird around here, aren't they?"

"So it would seem, my friend," I replied. For the next hour or so we just sat in silence staring at the side of the Kiches' house. Every once in a while we would glance over at each and then look back at the house next door.

Finally, Roger asked, "Do you think they will find out the truth?"

"What do you mean by the truth?" I asked.

"You know, the alien things," he said.

"Just keep your trap shut about any alien things," I said. "Got it?"

"Yeh, yeh, you don't have to worry," he tried to reassure me.

Of course, I knew better. His granny knew that he had smoked cigarettes (could smell it on him). His granny knew that he had been looking at naughty magazines (he went around looking pleased too often). His granny knew that his best friend told him stories to scare him. What Roger didn't know was that his granny was the epitome of a paranoiac schizophrenic! Two to three years of food and who knows what else stored up in her house! And what about telling the neighbors that I was a delusional drug taking weirdo! I would like to give her something to be paranoiac about! I knew that Roger loved his granny, but if the reptilian alien things had her for dinner it certainly wouldn't bother me.

"Listen, man," Roger said, "I snuck out to see you and I better be getting back before Granny wakes up."

"No, problem," I said. "Thanks for coming over and keeping me company for a while. Maybe we can hang out again sometime."

"That would be great," he said. "Gotta run."

"Watch your back, man," I said as he scurried off back to his house. The rest of the day was as boring as it had started out. I went in the house on occasion to raid the fridge, but returned to my guard post on the steps until my parents got home from work. I told them about my extremely boring day and that absolutely nothing had happened all day, especially next door. Dad wanted me to keep manning my post until the police removed the yellow tape surrounding the Kiches' property. I went to bed that night making plans in my head to do more than sit around all day the next day watching an empty house.

Chapter Thirty-two

After breakfast I got the dishes washed quickly and got to my guard post before my parents emerged from the house to head off to work. Dad once again warned me about crossing the yellow tape, but to keep a close eye on things again that day. I told him I wasn't too happy about losing money to put toward my car when I turned sixteen and he said he would make up for it if I just did as I was told. I assured him that I would and then he was off to work. Mom left about thirty minutes later for her bus and reiterated what Dad had said.

My plan for the day was to stay at my guard post for about an hour and then, making sure that no one was watching, I planned to violate the yellow tape and go exploring. Of course, that depended on whether or not the cops showed back up. That really hadn't occurred to me after I went to bed, but I was starting to worry about them showing up and ruining my plans. Then I started thinking about what would happen if I was snooping around over there and the cops showed up while I was doing my investigation. Mom hadn't been gone for more than fifteen minutes when I decided that if I was going to do any snooping around at the Kiches', I had better get going. I walked down to the end of the driveway to see if anyone was out and about and saw at least two of our neighbors pulling out of their driveways to head off to work. Since I hadn't seen anyone the day before I found this to be rather interesting, but dismissed it as I was more concerned at this point in getting a peek inside the Kiches house. I stood at the end of the driveway as both cars passed by and waved to both men driving the cars. Both of them only gave me a mean looking stare and sped off down the street. Dang Roger's grandmother! At that thought I glanced over at Roger's house to see if anyone was peeking out through the curtains and it looked very quiet over there. I sauntered around to the backyard and glanced up and down the other backyards to see if anyone was out hanging up laundry or anything else. Seeing no activity in the backyards on my side of the alley I looked across the alley to the backyards on the next street and not seeing any activity over there either I decided it was time to act.

I walked back to the area between our storage shed and the Kiches' storage shed and then slipped under the yellow tape and pressed my back up flat against the wall of their shed. I had often thought that someday I would like to be a secret agent. What I wanted to do next was slip around the corner and go to the back door of the Kiches' house. I figured I could peek in the window and see what the cop had been talking about since that door also went into their kitchen. I moved slowly along the wall and around the corner until I ended up next to the back door. I still didn't see anyone in any of the backyards so I turned and peeked into the kitchen cupping my hands around my face to get rid of the glare. Mrs. Kiches' had never put a curtain on the backdoor window, which I thought was kind of odd because everyone put curtains on their windows. I was actually shaking a little as I saw the dark areas on the kitchen floor that must have been the blood Sergeant Morgan had told us about.

So far it seemed that maybe he was telling the truth and maybe something really bad had happened to the Kiches. I knew there wasn't any chance of getting inside because the doors would all be locked, but I just had to try the door anyway. I reached out slowly to grab the doorknob as if it were a snake or something that would strike out and bite me. I slowly turned the knob and much to my surprise it turned and the door opened. It was such a shock that I quickly moved back to my position flat against the house. Had the cops screwed up and forgotten to lock the door or was there already someone in there prowling around? Quite frankly, the second idea worried me too much for me to continue my investigation and I reached over and closed the door. I checked the backyards again and still didn't see anyone so I scampered around the corner of the house, jumped over the yellow tape this time, and returned to our carport parking my butt on the steps.

I had just barely sat down on the steps when our kitchen door bumped me in the back. I let out a little scream and jumped halfway across the carport turning quickly to face whatever was coming out of our house. My mom came out the door and stood there with her hands on her hips staring at me. "Where have you been?" she asked me rather sternly.

"You sacred the crap out of me," I responded.

"I asked you a question," she said.

"I just went around to the backyard to make sure everything was ok," I lied. "Did you miss your bus?"

"Well, I have now because I had to come back to the house to get my name tag that I left on the kitchen counter this morning," she explained. "I called Mr. Tolison at work and told him what happened and that I would be late. You just make sure that you don't go across that yellow tape prowling around. You know how your curiosity gets you in trouble."

"Yes, ma'am," I promised.

"I know it's boring, but you have to keep an eye on our house," she told me.

"Yes, ma'am," I promised again.

Mom headed back up the street to the corner to catch the next bus to town and I settled back on the steps thinking that I just barely dodged another one. "Thank you, Jesus," I muttered out loud. For whatever reason I glanced over toward Roger's house and there was his grandmother standing on her front porch looking at me and shaking her head.

"WHAT?" I yelled across the street. She only kept shaking her head as she turned and went back in her house. *How much had she seen? Had she been watching the whole time while I was snooping next door? If she had, would she tell my parents about it? Of course she would! She was as big a gossip as Mrs. Kiches.* I was just about to get up and march over there to tell her to mind her own business and quit telling people I was a drug taking weirdo when two cop cars pulled up to the curb in front of the Kiches' with their lights flashing. Four cops got out of the two cars, but Sergeant Morgan wasn't one of them. They looked over at me and I waved hello and they waved back before unlocking the front door and entering the Kiches' house. A few minutes later one of the cops, the youngest looking one, came back outside and took up his own guard position at the corner of the house. I just kept sitting there staring at the house next door and listening as intently as I could, hoping to hear something. The young cop standing at the corner glanced over at me every few minutes. I guessed that he was supposed to keep an eye on me and make sure that I didn't do anything suspicious.

I might not have been too bright about some things, but I was smart enough not to arouse any suspicions with the cops when they were watching me so closely. After standing there for about thirty minutes without hardly moving the young cop started pacing up and down the driveway, but he was closely watching me every time he turned around and came back in my direction. The other three cops were inside the house for nearly two hours before they came out, locked the front door, and left. They obviously had been looking for something or somebody. *HOLY CRAP!* I thought to myself. *Somebody had seen me prowling around and had called the cops.* I was willing to bet it was that old hag that Roger called granny. She had found yet another way to break up my friendship with Roger. The cops must have used a fine-tooth comb going over everything in the house again to have taken so long. It didn't look like they had brought anything out with them so my guess was that they had been finger printing again. I could only hope that they hadn't finger printed the back door knob. Maybe if they hadn't found anything they would discredit Roger's grandmother and she would start looking ridiculous. As they say, "Hope springs eternal."

Chapter Thirty-three

There was still some time before my parents would be home, but I was supposed to stand guard and keep an eye on our house. I figured, however, that since the cops had already come and gone that it would be ok if I went inside and watched some television. True, I wouldn't be watching the outside of the house, but what were the cops going to find on the outside of our house? And my close call of almost getting caught inside the yellow tape around the Kiches' house made me think twice about going back over there, even though the cops had already been there. With my luck, they would be back about two seconds after I stepped inside the back door and would be surrounding the house because old lady Maleway had called them again informing them that an intruder was snooping around the Kiches' house. No sir, I wasn't going back over there as long as Roger's grandmother was alive! So, I went back into our house and settled down on the floor close in front of the television so I could constantly change the channels until I found something I wanted to watch.

After running through all three channels several times I decided to just watch the soap opera on the channel that was coming in the best. I had been lying there on the floor in front of the television, propped up on two sofa cushions, for about an hour when I heard a distant siren. Initially, I thought it sounded like a fire truck, but as it got louder and louder I realized that it was a police car. My first thought was that there had been a wreck nearby and I was stuck at our house and couldn't go see what all the commotion was about. I would always get on my bicycle and try to find where the sirens were going or where they had stopped. It was a big thrill to a young teenage boy with only one good friend in the neighborhood, one whose grandmother wouldn't let him hang out with me anymore, to chase sirens to see what was happening, especially when it was close to where I lived. I got up and turned the television off and went outside in the driveway to listen and see if I could figure out where the siren might be heading. Much to my surprise the "siren" now sounded like several sirens and they seemed to be coming in my direction.

Oh crap! I thought. *Could they be coming back to arrest me because they had found my fingerprints all over the backdoor doorknob?* I didn't know at that time that the cops had to have your prints on file to be able to match them to prints found at crime scenes. As soon as I saw the first cop car turn the corner at the end of our street I turned and ran back inside the house and locked the door. I ran to the front door to make sure it was locked, too. I got down on my hands and knees and crawled over to one of the front windows and parted the curtains about an inch so I could see where the cop cars were going. I just knew that they were coming after me, but much to my relief they kept going down the street and pulled up in front of Mrs. Chyspo's house. About thirty seconds later a small fire truck and an ambulance came roaring down the street and came to a screeching halt in front of the same house. Since they obviously weren't after me, I ventured back out onto the driveway and walked down to the street to see if I could figure out what was going on.

There were cops and firemen and emergency medical guys rushing around everywhere. I figured something must have happened to Mrs. Chyspo and one of the neighbors closer to her house had called the cops and ambulance. Then I remembered my encounter with that woman and the fact that she was really one of the reptilian alien things. I wanted to warn the cops and firemen, to tell them not to go in, but that would only make me look ridiculous. Especially if Mrs. Chyspo didn't turn into the alien thing. Maybe the police were called because someone went into her house and found the remains of the Kiches! But if that was true, then that meant the Kiches weren't alien things. This was becoming way too confusing and complicated.

I ventured closer down the street not letting our house get out of my sight. I just had to know what was going on down the street. I got within about one house of the excitement when a cop walked over to me and told me to keep my distance if I knew what was good for me. I asked him if I could stay where I was and he said yes, but not to get any closer. I assured him that I wouldn't, but I was concerned about Mrs. Chyspo (that of course being a lie). He told me that Mrs. Chyspo was fine. It was Mrs. Maleway that was injured.

"Roger's granny?!" I both asked and exclaimed at the same time. "What happened to Roger's granny?"

"Well, that's none of your business right now," he replied. "Now where does this Roger live?"

"Across the street from me," I said and pointed toward Mrs. Maleway's house.

"Do you know if Roger is there now?" the cop asked me.

"He's almost always there, except when his mother comes and gets him," I answered.

"Thanks, kid," the cop replied and started off toward Mrs. Maleway's house.

I watched as the cop walked up to the front door and knocked. There must not have been an answer, because he knocked again and once again after a couple of minutes had passed. He came walking back down the street toward me and when he got back to where I was still standing he asked me if I knew where Roger's mother lived. I didn't, because Roger had never told me and I was never really interested in where his mother lived.

"Does Roger have a telephone in that house?" he asked me.

"Yes, sir," I answered and gave him the number at Mrs. Maleway's house. After writing it down on a small pad he walked away toward his patrol car and got in on the driver's side. I figured he was going to call the number and see if anyone would answer. After a couple of minutes he got out of the car, looked in my direction and shook his head and went back inside Mrs. Chyspo's house. I figured that Roger was probably inside and scared to death that all the police were around, thus he wasn't going to answer the door or the telephone. I kept my position in front of Mrs. Chyspo's neighbor's house hoping to see something when the cops and firemen and ambulance guys came out.

I was also keeping a constant watch on our house, because it would be a perfect ploy for the cops to use to sneak into our house behind my back while all the commotion was going on down the street. About every ten seconds I looked one direction and then back in the other direction. After about thirty minutes of this I thought my neck was going to twist right off because my shoulder muscles were beginning to ache. I was just about to give it up and go back to our driveway and watch from there since that would be easier on my neck when two firemen came out of the house carrying a stretcher with Roger's grandmother on it. She was strapped down and seemed to be bleeding from her head, which was wrapped in white bandages, but the blood was seeping through.

Holy crap! I thought again. *What could have happened in Mrs. Chyspo's house? Why was Roger's grandmother at her house in the first place? Where was Roger? Why wasn't he at his granny's like he always was?* I seemed to have a thousand questions and not one answer. At that point another cop started walking up the street toward me. When he got to me he told me that Roger's mother had picked him up the night before and he just wanted me to know where my friend was so I wouldn't worry about him. I thanked him and then asked about Mrs. Maleway. The cop said that there had been a little confrontation between her and Mrs. Chyspo inside the house and Mrs. Chyspo seems to have struck Mrs. Maleway in the head with an iron skillet, but Roger's grandmother was going to be ok. She only seemed to have a small cut on her head and maybe a slight concussion.

"By the way," the cop said as he started to walk away, "the argument they had seems to have been about you."

"Me?" I said questioningly. "What do you mean, about me?"

"Can't say for sure," he told me, "but that's Mrs. Chyspo's story. I'll let you know if I find out more."

"Thanks," I said, and the cop walked back down the street to Mrs. Chyspo's house.

Ok, this was more intriguing than the Kiches' disappearance. What could they have been arguing about me for? Who started the argument? Once again, I had a thousand questions and not one answer. Well, I did know that the confrontation was about me. That made me feel both important and scared at the same time. I had a lot of thinking to do and there was only one place for that, the doorstep at the kitchen door.

Chapter Thirty-four

Sitting on the doorstep was where Mom found me when she got home. I was so lost in my thoughts that I didn't even see her walk up the driveway. She took me by the shoulder and shook me waking me up from my wide-eyed daydream. When we were inside she asked me if there had been any activity that day and I related the excitement about Roger's grandmother and Mrs. Chyspo, leaving out, of course, the part about their argument being about me. I figured they would find that out soon enough if the cops came back around.

When Dad got home I had to relate the story again word for word just exactly like I had told it to Mom. He said that it wasn't any surprise to him that old lady Maleway had finally got her due for spreading so much untrue gossip about people; Mrs. Maleway who never missed church and always drug Roger along with her. Mom didn't argue that point with him, but said that she hoped Roger's grandmother would be ok just the same. Dad said he guessed that was the Christian thing to wish for, but that the devil would catch up to her one day. Understand that my parents never went to church nor insisted that I go, but there weren't any people around more God-fearing than my parents.

There wasn't any more talk about the incident that happened that day or about the Kiches' disappearance. As usual, all three of us just settled down in front of the television for the evening with Dad snoring and Mom crocheting. Around 9:30 Mom woke up Dad and told us both we better get to bed, because tomorrow was another workday and we needed our rest. I knew there wasn't any need to argue with her about staying up any later, because she just wouldn't have it. However, there were some nights that she didn't get to bed before eleven o'clock. Even though she had worked hard all day, being on her feet the whole time, she came home, fixed dinner, and often did ironing or sewing or even the wash if it was piling up.

I got ready for bed and crawled in feeling more tired than I thought. I must have fallen asleep right away, because I don't remember hearing Mom out in the kitchen either working at the old Singer sewing machine or getting the squeaky old ironing board out of the closet. Sometime during the night or wee hours of the morning I sat straight up in bed wide awake, thinking that I had heard a loud growl outside my window. I sat there wide-eyed and my ears perked up waiting to hear the sound again and at the same time hoping that I didn't. No such luck! The growl was even louder and sounded very close to my window now. There was a clear sky and a full moon that night and I would have sworn on two stacks of Bibles, including the one Mrs. Root Beer Lady gave me, that there were ominous shadows lurking at my bedroom window. There weren't any trees in our backyard, so that couldn't be used as an excuse. The shadows seemed to take on the silhouettes of the reptilian alien things and I was starting to sweat a little, but I couldn't find my voice to call out to my parents.

Then the shapes seemed to all come together as one huge shape and that shape turned to show a silhouette in profile and its huge mouth opened wide and growled so loud that I knew it must have woken my parents up, but I didn't hear any movement from their bedroom across the hall. The dark shape outside my window now turned back to face the window and its large claw-like hands grasped at the bottom of the window trying to raise it. This monster was trying to get into my bedroom and I knew that if it did I was a goner! I finally found my voice and yelled for my dad. I still didn't hear any movement from their bedroom and I yelled even louder, although I could barely hear myself. The thing outside my window seemed to be agitated by my yelling and started clawing more feverishly at my window to get in. I was too scared to move so I kept yelling as loud as I could that something was trying to break into the house through my bedroom window. Mom came plodding into my room wanting to know what all the commotion was about and all I could do was point at the window while I sat bolt upright shaking like a leaf!

"What?" Mom asked, sounding very irritated.

"Outside my window," I finally got out. "Someone's trying to get in my room!"

"I don't see anyone at your window," she said. "Were you having a bad nightmare?"

"NO!" I yelled. "They're trying to get in and get me!"

"They who?" she calming inquired although I could tell she was still irritated.

"How should I know?" I answered. "All I know is that something was trying to get in my window!"

"Now it's something," she said. "What kind of something is trying to get in?"

"I don't know," I lied, fully aware that it had to be the reptilian alien things. "Something, someone, whatever, it's trying to get in. It was scratching at my window and trying to open it!"

"Am I going to have to wake your father up and let him deal with this?" she asked me.

"If he will do something about it," I basically sassed back, which wasn't the right thing to do with my mother.

"You sass me one more time, young man, and I'll have your father take his wide leather belt to you," she stated matter-of-factly.

"I'm not sassing you," I sassed back. "But I can't sleep with something or someone prowling around outside my window all night." At that remark she turned around and went back to her bedroom. In about thirty seconds Dad came into my room carrying his wide leather belt.

"Would you like to tell me why I have been wakened up in the middle of the night?" he asked me.

I related my story to him and begged him to go outside and check it out. He said he would, but if he didn't find anything he was going to wear my skinny little butt out when he came back inside. I knew that was the truth and almost changed my mind about him going outside to check out my story, but at that point I was willing to get a whipping if it meant knowing that nothing was still lurking outside my window. He went back to his bedroom and put on some trousers and shoes and then ventured outside with a flashlight and his .38 revolver, "just in case." He hadn't been outside for more than a minute when I heard him exclaim loudly, "HOLY CRAP!" The next thing I heard was three loud bangs from his .38 revolver. Mom and I were both out of bed and down the hall in a flash. I was out the door first, but she was hot on my heels. I had grabbed another flashlight I had near my bed and was shining it down the back of the house. Mom was hanging over my shoulder and for the first time in my life I felt like she was more scared than me and was behind me for protection.

My flashlight beam shone on Dad and I called out, "Dad, what's going on? Are you ok?"

"I'm fine son. You two come over here and look at this," he directed. We both walked along the back of the house until we were standing next to Dad. "Look at this," he said pointing at the ground with his flashlight. The light was falling across the body of what looked like a really, really big dog. "Darndest thing I've ever seen," he said sounding bewildered. "Do you know what this is?"

"A really, really big dog?" I said.

"This is no dog, James," he said. "This is a wolf, and the biggest one I've ever seen and I saw a few big ones back in Tennessee when I was growing up."

"A wolf?" Mom asked. "Where would a wolf come from around here?"

"That's the sixty-four thousand dollar question," Dad said. "But I promise you this is a wolf." He then moved his flashlight beam to the bottom of the window frame outside my bedroom. "I guess you were telling the truth about this thing trying to get in. Look at those huge scratches on the bottom of the window."

"YES!" I exclaimed with glee in my voice.

"What?" Dad said turning to me.

"Nothing," I replied. "It's just that I knew I wasn't having a nightmare."

"Well, I guess not," he replied.

I helped Dad get a big packing blanket wrapped around the dead wolf while Mom held the flashlight and we drug it back around to the carport, because it was too heavy to lift, and locked the body in the storage shed until the next morning. Dad said that he and I would take the animal down to the game warden's office first thing in the morning and turn it over to him. "Let him worry about what to do with it," he said. We went back inside and back to bed until the next morning, but even though the danger seemed to be dead I still didn't get much sleep that night. I kept dreaming about shadows lurking at my bedroom window.

Chapter Thirty-five

The next morning I helped Dad load the large packing blanket bundle into the trunk of the car and rode with him down to the game warden's office. When the game warden saw it he said the same thing Dad had said, "Holy crap! Where in thunderation did you find this thing?"

"Lurking outside my son's bedroom window around 2:00 this morning," Dad answered. "It was trying to claw its way into his bedroom."

"Holy crap!" the game warden said again. "I've seen some big wolves in my time, but this one is the biggest I've ever seen!"

"Same here," dad said. "Where do you think it came from?"

"That's the sixty-four thousand dollar question," the game warden said.

"That sounds familiar," I mumbled.

"Huh?" asked the game warden.

"Nothing," Dad answered for me and gave me a stern look.

"I thought that you would know what to do with this thing, so I brought it in," dad offered.

"Thanks! Thanks a lot!" the game warden said facetiously.

"You're welcome," Dad said mockingly.

"Oh, you're a barrel of monkeys," the game warden replied.

"What exactly does that mean?" I asked matter-of-factly. Both men turned and gave me that stern "who asked you to speak" look. "Ok, ok. I'll be quiet."

"So, what do you think you'll do with this thing?" Dad asked again.

"Well, first thing I'll do is put it in the freezer and then try to figure out where it came from and what we should do with it after that. Maybe the local museum would want to take it and get it stuffed to put on display," the game warden offered.

"That sounds like a really good plan," Dad agreed. "Well, I guess we'll be getting back to work. Let me know if you decide to give it to the museum so we can go down and see it sometime. And I'd really like to know how it ended up in our backyard last night."

"That's a big ten-four," the game warden said and Dad and I got back in the car and headed off to the service station. I didn't even question going to the station because I was still pretty shook up from the whole incident and really didn't want to be alone at the house.

"Hey, Dad, what's the game warden's name anyway?" I asked as he drove along Memorial Boulevard toward the service station.

"Mr. Fish," Dad said and I started laughing so hard tears were forming in my eyes.

When I could catch my breath I asked, "His first name isn't Snook, is it?"

At that we both started laughing so hard that Dad had a hard time keeping the car in his lane, but we weren't far from the station and we did arrive safely. We were both still giggling when we got out of the car and opened up the station for business that day.

"You don't mind spending the day here with me, do you," Dad asked.

"Are you kidding?" I said. "You couldn't pay me enough to stay home alone today."

"That's what I thought," Dad replied. "Why don't you get some sand and start scrubbing on those oil stains on the driveway out by the ethyl pump?" Dad told me more than asked.

"I'm on it," I said and got the bag of sand and started on the oil stains. The day went by without much excitement except that the girl at the "burger joint" across the street came prancing over around lunchtime with a bag of burgers and fries. She said that her father sent the food over for free because we were good customers and he wanted it to stay that way. Dad thanked her and as she turned to leave she stopped, turned back around, looked right at me (and you know I was already watching this little angel start to walk away), and said, "I get off at three so I can do my homework from summer school. Would you like to help me with it?"

I turned, looked at Dad and he nodded, turned back to her wide-eyed and in my best nervous voice said, "Sure. Love to."

"Well, then, I'll see you around three. I study in the backroom where my father has his office," she explained.

"I . . . I'll . . . I'll be there then," I said in my best stutter.

"By the way, my name's Cookie," she said in what must have been the most beautiful voice that anyone on the planet had ever heard.

"My name's Ja . . . James," I stuttered.

"Bye, James. See you later," Cookie said and she turned and walked away.

"Well, well," Dad said. "How long have you two been ogling each other?"

"That's the first time she's ever even acknowledged that I exist," I explained.

"Oh, my shy son," Dad said. "What am I ever going to do with you?"

"Take me to a doctor to help me with my stutter," I replied and Dad starting laughing again, which became contagious as I started laughing again as well.

When three o'clock rolled around I was already standing at the front counter inquiring if Cookie was ready for me to help her with her homework. Her dad looked me up and down and told me if I wasn't my dad's son he'd chase me off with a bucket of hot grease. He let me know in no uncertain terms that I was to be really, really nice to his little girl if I knew what was good for me. I assured him that my intentions were only to help her with her homework, but I would like to be friends with Cookie if that was ok with him. That seemed to please him and he showed me to his office where Cookie already had her books laid out on his desk waiting for my expert help. As it turned out, she was having to repeat an algebra course that summer that she had failed in the Spring term and was still having trouble with understanding it. Now, the one thing that was probably my best subject throughout school had been math and algebra came easy to me. As a matter-of-fact, I had made straight A's throughout school in most of my subjects, but especially in math. There surely had to be a God in Heaven to have dropped this little beauty into my life who needed help with math! My confidence rose several notches as I proclaimed, "Ah, math! My specialty! Let's get down to work!"

Chapter Thirty-six

"James, I've been wanting to meet you for a long time, but my dad doesn't like me talking to boys," Cookie said as I walked around to her side of the desk where she had a chair waiting for me. "I told Dad that I had heard you were really good in math and that I could certainly use the help. Because your dad is a good customer he agreed for me to ask you to help me. That's why I brought the burgers and fries over earlier. It was the only way I could figure out to meet you. I hope you don't mind my boldness and being so sneaky."

"Not at all, Cookie," I replied. "I have wanted to meet you for a long time, too, but I'm kind of shy around girls."

"Oh, you're just being silly," she said. "There are lots of girls at school who would love to be your girlfriend, because you're always so nice and polite."

"That's kind of you to say, Cookie," I said. "Does that include you?"

"Now, that's not being shy," she told me, and, "yes, that includes me."

"Wow!" was all I could come up with at that moment.

Cookie saw my face turning red and said, "Do you want me to be your girlfriend?"

"Wow!" I said again. "That would be a dream come true!"

"What would be a dream come true?" she asked me.

"You being my girlfriend," I replied.

"Well then, don't you have a question for me?" Cookie asked in a soft sexy voice with her head tilted slightly down, but her eyes looking up at me.

For a few seconds my mind just wouldn't work and then it came to me that she wanted me to ask her to be my girlfriend. "Cookie, I would love for you to be my girlfriend," I started. "Would you go steady with me? I'll get you a friendship ring as soon as I can get downtown to the store where my mom works."

"James," she replied, I would absolutely love to be your steady girlfriend. I'll be the envy of lots of girls"

"You're just saying that, but I appreciate it, especially coming from you," I said.

"Silly, boy," Cookie said in that soft sexy voice.

Of course, she could have sounded like our gruff old science teacher, Mr. Trischmey, and I would have thought it was sexy. All I could think was, *Dear God, please don't let this be a dream.*

Cookie said, "Now, we need to pretend that you're helping me with my math homework in case my dad pokes his nosey little head in to check on us."

"Oh, I'll do anything I can to help you get a good grade in math," I said in my most sincere voice.

"I didn't set this up to get help on my math, silly," Cookie said. "I did it to get to meet you so that I could find out if you liked me as much as I like you."

"But didn't you fail math last term?" I asked.

"Yes, but that's because I really don't like math," Cookie told me matter-of-factly. "I'm doing much better in summer school. As a matter-of-fact, I have a "B" right now and might even bring that up to an "A" if I do some extra credit. But don't tell my dad, because he doesn't know that I'm doing that good. I told him I was having trouble because I wanted us to get together."

"You're the most awesome girl I've ever known," I said and blushed. "I think I'm falling in love."

"And you say you don't know why a lot of girls like you," she told me. "Now sit down here next to me and let's pretend to be studying. I've already worked on a lot of problems, but Dad only saw an empty piece of paper the last time he came back to check on me." Cookie pulled out the papers from the back of her notebook and laid them around like we had been working on the problems together.

I was sitting on her right side and after I sat down I laid my arm across the back of her chair and after a few seconds of sitting and gazing into each other's eyes I let my arm slip down around her shoulders and gave her a little hug. Cookie then leaned forward and gave me a little kiss right on the lips! *Oh God, please don't let this be a dream,* I thought again. I didn't know much about women yet, but I was sure the look of love in Cookie's eyes was real. We heard some heavy footsteps coming toward the back room and we quickly scooted a little apart. I pretended to be explaining a problem to Cookie when her father came into the room to check on us.

"How's it going back here?" he asked in a deep voice.

"Great!" I exclaimed. "Cookie's catching on real fast. She has already worked a few problems."

Her dad looked back and forth between us a couple of times and said, "I'll be danged! You might just have to become a regular fixture around if her grades improve."

"You make the best hamburgers anywhere," I said in my best complimentary voice.

He just chuckled, turned and walked out of the room. Then he popped his head back in the room and said, "Heck, you two might just become high school sweethearts."

"Oh, daddy," Cookie said and we both blushed.

"Back to that math," he said and winked at us and then once again left the room.

As soon as he was gone we took each other's hand and kissed again. Wondering if maybe her dad knew what was going on, I asked Cookie, "Do you think he's wise to us already?"

"Knowing my daddy, he probably saw it written all over us," she answered. "But, he must like you or he would have thrown you in the garbage can out back."

We started giggling as quietly as we could and when we settled down Cookie got a few more problems worked, with my help this time, which made the problem solving go a little faster. We didn't get too much accomplished on her math problems, however, because we wanted to have a reason for me to come over every day, if possible. Every few minutes we gazed at each other and kissed and then went back to the math problems. After about another thirty minutes we heard some footsteps again and separated an appropriate distance. This time it was my dad saying that it was time to head home and wanted to know how long we would be. Cookie told him that we could come to a stopping point if I could come over again tomorrow to help her some more.

"Sounds like this could get to be a habit," Dad said and winked at me. Cookie and I both blushed. Dad continued, "Well, there's not much summer left and I guess James could come to work with me everyday instead of mowing yards so he could come over and help you with your homework in the afternoons. Are you sure it's ok with your dad?"

At that moment Cookie's dad walked up and said as he placed a hand on my dad's shoulder, "It's fine with me as long as it's your boy. Seems like a fine young man."

"Well, most of the time he's pretty good," dad said.

"Dad!" I exclaimed.

"I wouldn't trade him for anybody else's two sons," Dad said.

Both men turned and walked out of the room chuckling while Cookie and I just sat there turning red. One more quick kiss and we said bye and Dad and I headed for home.

On the way home dad said, "This is going to be very interesting to your mother."

"I'm sure," I replied and we drove the rest of the way in silence.

Chapter Thirty-seven

After my mom got the whole story about Cookie and me she was smiling from ear to ear, but then she got serious and asked me, "What about Leasure?" Oh crap, I thought. In the presence of a beauty like Cookie who obviously liked me and who pursued me, I hadn't even thought about my other girlfriend.

"I gave this some serious thought on the way home tonight," I lied. All I had thought about was Cookie and where our next encounter might take us. "I'm going to break the news to Leasure tomorrow. I'll call her from the station, if that's ok with you, Dad."

Dad nodded his approval and said, "I was wondering why you were so quiet all the way home," and winked at me.

"Leasure's been acting kind of funny lately anyway," I offered. "I think her mother doesn't really like me. Leasure told me the last time she was over here that her mother hoped she would marry a doctor or lawyer someday. You know that doesn't mean me!"

"You know, I've never really cared that much for that woman," my mom said. "I've complimented her on so many things and she has never once returned a compliment. And she always acts like she's better than us when she and her husband are around. Always talking about how much money her insurance salesman husband is making and that's why she doesn't have to work and has three little brats!"

"Did she call them that?" I asked. At that we all three cracked up and started laughing.

"If she's lucky, her little harlot will marry a garbage collector!" Mom said. "I'm glad that you're finally seeing the light and dumping Leasure. You and Cookie will make such a cute couple."

"Oh, Mom," I said blushing.

Then Dad chimed in with, "Why don't we go out to eat tonight? Sort of a celebration to honor our son becoming a man."

We both looked at Dad like he had lost his mind, because he NEVER wanted to go out to eat, except when he was at work, of course.

"What?" he asked. "I like to eat out sometimes. Just not a buffet." Dad didn't like buffets because it meant him having to carry his own tray and that was somewhat of a problem. When Dad was in his early twenties he had entered the army. One day when he started to clean his gun it went off and he shot himself through the palm of his right hand. The bullet went clean through breaking bones and blowing the flesh off the back of his hand. Since he was right-handed that turned out to be a real problem. He never regained the use of his right hand and had to learn to write all over again with his left hand. He could hold a wrench between his thumb and the side of his hand and he could pinch the fire out of you with the same, but dad had a problem holding a tray in his left hand and dipping up food with his right. He never did learn to use his right hand for eating with a fork or spoon.

"Where did you have in mind?" mom asked dad.

"The A&W Drive-In stays open late. How about that?" Dad stated more than asked. That way we could eat in the car.

"Sounds great to me," I offered. "Can I get a foot-long chili dog and fries?"

"You, young man, can have anything you want," Dad said.

"Well then," Mom said, "let's get going. I'm hungry, too. Do you think Cookie would like to go with us?" she asked looking at me.

"Really?" I asked. "You wouldn't mind?"

"Not at all," mom answered. "Do you know her number at the restaurant?"

"Yes, but wouldn't that seem kind of strange?" I asked. "I mean, we're going out to eat, but not at her dad's place."

"I don't think Mr. Morgan would mind in a case like this," Dad chimed in.

"Ok, I'll call her and see if she can go with us," I said. I went to the telephone by the kitchen door and sat down on the telephone bench and dialed the number at Mr. Morgan's restaurant. All of a sudden it had become a restaurant instead of a "burger joint." Mr. Morgan answered the telephone and I told him who I was and asked if I could speak to Cookie. He said sure and called Cookie to the telephone. I told her what was up and she asked her dad for permission and he said yes and I was about to go on my first "date" with Cookie. My heart was racing so fast I could hardly talk when I got off the phone, but my parents got the gist of my stammering and we took off to pick up Cookie. I was freaking out! I was going on a date with Cookie and we were going to be sitting next to each other on the back seat of my dad's car and probably holding hands and I might even sneak a kiss and I was freaking out to be going on a date with Cookie! Did I mention that? I knew now that there had to be a God and I was going to start praying and giving thanks a heck of a lot more!

On the way over to pick up Cookie, I started thinking about the fact that nothing weird had happened to me that day. No reptilian alien things had tried to get me or even come around where I was and there weren't any wolves prowling around the station. Maybe Cookie was my good luck charm. Cookie was definitely good luck! Never in my wildest dreams, and I had had a few about Cookie, did I ever think that I would be going steady with Cookie. It was going to be good to be rid of Leasure and to walk around school in a few weeks with Cookie hanging on to my arm. *Every guy at school would stare in disbelief! James was going steady with Cookie! Thank you, God!*

Cookie came running out of her dad's restaurant as Dad pulled up close to the front door. When the car had stopped, I jumped out and held the door open for Cookie. She thanked me as she slid about halfway across the back seat and waited for me to slide in next to her. When I had gotten back in the car she said she was so excited that I had asked her to go out with us and she thanked my mom and dad for letting her come along.

"There's no better time than the present for the two of you to start dating," Mom said causing me to turn a nice bright shade of red.

"I totally agree," Cookie said, as she took my hand and squeezed it. Then she scooted as close to me as she could get without pushing me up against the car door. I removed my hand from hers and put my arm around her shoulders and she moved even closer, although I didn't think it was possible.

Dad asked Cookie if the A&W was ok and she gave a resounding, "Absolutely! I just love the A&W! My dad actually takes us there about once a week because he just loves the chili dogs there and so do I."

This just has to be a dream. "Those are my favorite, too," I chimed in. "I bet we have a lot more in common, too!"

"I'm absolutely sure we do, James," Cookie said giving me that little look that would drive me crazy over the rest of my life – that is, providing we stayed together forever. After that comment we just sat snuggled up as close as possible on the back seat until we got to the A&W.

Dad parked the car and we waited for the carhop to come out and take our order. After we ordered my mom engaged Cookie in a conversation that basically revolved around how long Cookie had had her eye on me. Mom and Cookie chattered back and forth as if they had been best friends forever. Dad and I just sat and stared into space pretending not to listen, but mom knew we were both taking in every word that was exchanged between the girls. Our food finally came and after we had eaten we had to take Cookie back to her dad's restaurant since it was getting close to closing time and Cookie had to help clean up before they went home. I walked Cookie back to the front door and we snuck a little kiss and said goodnight.

As Cookie was going through the door she turned and said to me, "I'm already looking so forward to tomorrow."

"Me, too," I replied. "Cookie?" I said.

"Yes," she said.

"Would it be too soon for me to say that I think I love you?" I asked.

She turned toward me, took two quick steps back in my direction, and nearly knocked me over as she threw her arms around me and said, "Of course not! I love you, too, silly. Now, I've really got to get inside and help dad. Goodnight." She gave me another little kiss and I stood there like a zombie watching her disappear into the restaurant. Dad honked the horn to jolt me out of my stupor. I got back in the car and we drove home with Mom and Dad quietly giggling the entire way home, but not kidding me about the evening.

Chapter Thirty-eight

"James! James! James, wake up!" my dad was practically shouting at me.

"Huh?" I said as I raised my head up off the desk in the service station office.

"You fell asleep at the desk while I was out in the garage working on Mr. Antonio's Buick," Dad explained. "I even had to wait on three cars that pulled in out front."

"I'm sorry," I offered.

"What were you dreaming about anyway?" dad asked. "You kept mumbling something about a cookie or something."

"Dreaming?" I asked. "No, no, no, NO! I couldn't have been dreaming! It was too real!"

"What was too real?" dad asked.

"My stupid dream," I answered sounding just as disappointed as I was.

"Want to tell me what you were dreaming about?" Dad asked.

"Girls. A girl. Across the street," I answered.

"Ah, Mr. Morgan's girl, Cookie," Dad said, understandingly.

"Yeh, Cookie," I said. "No chance for me there, huh?"

"I would guess no," dad said trying to sound sympathetic. "I think Cookie is a little out of your league, son. Sorry."

"Oh, it doesn't really matter," I responded. "Just a stupid dream."

"Well, now that you have had a good long nap, I think you need to get your butt up and get some cleaning done around here," Dad instructed.

"Yes, sir," I said and got back to my chores around the station. I couldn't believe that I had been dreaming all that business about Cookie, but I obviously had been dreaming. Oh well, it was a good dream while it lasted. *So much for praying,* I thought to myself. "God," I said more to myself than to anybody or anything that I thought might be God as I scrubbed the driveway, "couldn't this one dream have been real?" Cookie was more than just a 'little out of my league'. Cookie was major league and I was more like little league! Guess I would just stay with Leasure, even though I would never be a doctor or lawyer.

Then I started thinking about something else again. It had been a fairly uneventful day at the station, just like I had dreamed. Could it be that the station was off limits to the reptilian alien things? It was at that very moment that a 1962 Corvette convertible came screaming into the station and up to the pumps where I was scrubbing oil off the pavement with an old broom and sand. I heard a car coming and looked up just in time to jump out of the way. The Corvette squealed to a stop leaving a short line of rubber on the pavement that I would have to try and scrub up later. When I looked at the driver my heart nearly jumped out of my chest! Sitting there as pretty as ever was Monica! She motioned for me to come closer and knowing better, I still did just as she wished. I walked up to the driver's side door and peaked down to see what she was wearing. Monica had on a very short skirt and had it pulled up all the way to her skimpy little panties. Now, I thought that my heart, along with one other thing, was going to explode out of my pants, I mean chest.

"Bend over here close," Monica told me. "I want to whisper a little secret to you."

Again, I knew better, but I did as directed and bent way over so I could get a really good peak while she whispered whatever she wanted to me.

"GOTCHA!" she screeched as she grabbed me by the shirt and pulled me about half way into the car. At that moment my dad was coming around the corner of the building, having just been to the rest room.

"HEY, WHAT THE DEVIL'S GOING ON?" Dad yelled and came running out toward the Corvette as I was balancing on my stomach on the top of the car door. "LET GO OF MY KID!"

Monica jerked her head around and literally snarled at Dad, but also let go of me in the same movement. I fell backwards into the regular pump and ended up sitting on the curb surrounding the pumps. The Corvette screeched out of the station laying down a long line of rubber on the pavement, which I would have to clean up. Dad kept a little pad of paper in his front shirt pocket and had already pulled it out and was writing down the tag number on the Corvette. The Corvette was probably doing close to sixty as it pulled out of the driveway and into the path of an oncoming semi that had to swerve to keep from hitting it. The Corvette disappeared down Memorial Boulevard faster than anything that I had ever seen as Dad ran up to me to see if I was ok.

"What was that woman trying to do?" he asked, as he helped me to my feet.

"I guess she was trying to kidnap me," I answered shaking and a little unsteady on my feet. "She motioned for me to come over by the car door and then she grabbed me by my shirt and started pulling me into the car before I could do anything."

"Good thing I came out when I did," he stated matter-of-factly. "Well, I got her tag number and I'm going to call the police right now. Have any idea what model Corvette she was driving?"

"Great idea, dad," I said, thinking that finally the police could start looking for the reptilian alien things, even though they didn't know what they were getting into. "She was driving a 1962 Corvette," I announced proudly. "I know my Corvettes."

"That you do, son," Dad acknowledged. "Have you ever seen that woman before?"

I started to lie and say no, but thought better of it because if the police caught up to her and she didn't turn into a reptilian alien thing and kill and eat them, she would probably say that I had mowed her yard. "I've mowed her yard a couple of times," I confessed, "but she never tried anything before." As soon as that was out of my mouth I realized that was about as stupid as I could get. My problem was that I didn't have the ability to think past the words trying to come out of my mouth at any given moment. When the police found out that I had mowed her yard a couple of times they would want me to show them where her house was located.

"This is the very thing we moved here to get away from," Dad said. "It's hard to believe that people will stoop so low to try and steal other people's kids, especially in small towns like this." At that, Dad went straight to the station office and called the police. About thirty minutes later an unmarked police car pulled in and parked next to the building on the rest room side. Two detectives got out and came into the office where Dad and I were waiting. Over the next thirty to forty minutes they asked a lot of what seemed like unimportant questions, but I'm sure they had their reasons. A couple of times I had to go out and wait on customers, but they kept talking to Dad while I was out of the office.

After they left Dad told me they were going to put out an APB on the Corvette and hope to catch the woman who tried to kidnap me as soon as possible. They told Dad that she would probably strike again somewhere else since she had failed with me. *Oh, she's not through with me,* I thought. I only wish that I could have told my dad the whole horrible story, but then he would just think I was being paranoid – which I was! The amazing thing was that Dad didn't mention to them that I had mowed her yard a couple of times.

He later told me that he didn't want his son riding around in a police car for everybody and their half-brother to see.

Whew, I thought. *That was a close call.* I knew now that no place was safe from Monica or her friends. All I could hope for was that Dad would let me come to work with him the rest of the summer. Hopefully, when school started back there wouldn't be any problems with the creatures that were pursuing me. Hopefully they would all go back to planet Iguana, or wherever they were from. Then I had a really terrible thought: *what if this was actually their planet and we were experiments that had gone bad and we had been rebelling against the things that I have been calling alien? Or what if we were their slaves and they had lost control over us and the only way to regain that control is to kill and eat us?*

I was beginning to think that there were far more questions than answers. Then I had another terrible thought: *If we were their slaves, then the police probably worked for them, unless they, too, are reptilian alien things!* I didn't know how much more of this I could take. It would certainly be interesting to find out what the police had to say about my attempted kidnapping when they came back around. However, there was an upside to my attempted kidnapping this afternoon. I had gotten a great peek at Monica's panties, reptilian alien thing or not, and that was worth nearly being kidnapped! Those raging hormones always seemed to put everything into perspective for this fourteen-year-old young man.

Chapter Thirty-nine

It was a couple of days later when the police detectives came back around with some news, or I should say LOTS of news! First, they had actually found the 1962 Corvette convertible on another street about four or five blocks from our house. There was no sign of the woman who had tried to kidnap me, but the Corvette was sitting in an overgrown, empty field.

Second, Mrs. Chyspo had dropped any charges against Mrs. Maleway and had even picked her up from jail and took her home.

Those awful old witches! I thought. One had tried to kill and eat me and the other was keeping my best friend from having anything to do with me! *Those awful old witches!* I thought again.

Thirdly, there was news about the Kiches. It seems that Mrs. Kiches really was as unstable as we thought she might be and had found Mr. Kiches' .357 revolver while no one was home and committed suicide. The cops told my dad that she had put the gun in her mouth and pulled the trigger, which blew off the entire back of her head; thus, all the blood. Mr. Kiches had found out that Kelvin had "run away" and had been staying at a teacher friend's house for the past few days. After rearranging the teacher's nose, Mr. Kiches made Kelvin come back home with him, but when they got home what they found was Mrs. Kiches lying on the kitchen floor in a pool of blood. It had been too much for either of them to deal with and after the police located Mr. Kiches and Kelvin at a relative's house in Georgia, he told them that they would never return to that house again.

Now, to me, that only settled two mysteries: Kelvin's disappearance and what had happened at the

Kiches' house. *Where is Monica? Why has Mrs. Chyspo really dropped the charges against Roger's grandmother? And, are the cops really telling us the truth?* Once again, I had more questions than answers. The only good thing at this time was that nothing weird had happened over the past couple of days. I knew that the service station wasn't off limits to the reptilian alien things now, because Monica had been there and had tried to do me in a couple of days before. My plan until school started back in August was not to be out of yelling distance of my parents at any time. Roger wasn't coming around or calling me over to his house now and after my dream about Cookie I didn't care if I saw Leasure or not either. So much for what little "social life" I had, but if it meant not encountering the creatures pursuing me then I was a happy camper!

The only problem was that a couple of days after the cops had been back to tell us all their news, Dad had to run across town to the auto parts store to pick up a master cylinder for Mr. Antonio's car; Dad hadn't been able to work on his car the past few days because the auto parts store had to order the part. I was not very happy about this, but the auto parts store didn't deliver so there wasn't much choice. I told him to be careful, but please hurry! He said he could ask Mr. Morgan to come over and "help me hold down the fort," but I said no because that might turn out to be embarrassing. He said he understood, but if anyone acting strange came in while he was gone I was to lock myself in the storeroom. *No problem there!*

It usually took Dad about thirty minutes to go to the auto parts store and get back, but he was gone for over an hour this time because there was a bad wreck on Memorial Boulevard and he got caught in the middle of a block and couldn't detour. After about forty minutes had passed I started to get worried that maybe the reptilian alien things had gotten my dad and now they were going to come for me. Fortunately, only half of that happened, but that half happened to me! Remember the Cadillac that cruised by our house early in the summer with the old man, Mrs. Root Beer Lady, and Monica? I was sitting at the desk in the office twirling around in the office chair and getting pretty dizzy when that very same Cadillac pulled up next to the curb by the front door. The old man was driving and the old hag was on the passenger side in the front. I didn't see Monica in the car, but then she was probably hiding in the trunk.

The passenger side door flew open and the old hag exited the Caddy like a teenage boy who had just been offered a ride in a 1962 Corvette convertible with a gorgeous blond! The front door was propped open because it was summer and we didn't have an air conditioner in the office. I quit spinning almost as fast as the old hag came out of the car, but I was just dizzy enough to not be able to run very fast without bumping into things. As it turned out, that was actually a good thing as I knocked over the Gordon's potato chip rack and it fell right across the path into the office through the front door. I staggered out through the side door into the garage and as I was trying to run toward the storage room my head started to clear. I picked up my pace while the old hag was picking herself up off the floor from having stumbled over the potato chip rack.

As I opened the door to the storage room the Caddy pulled into the garage and plowed under the rear end of Mr. Antonio's car, which was slightly raised up on the lift because Dad was working on the brakes, bringing the Caddy to a halt. Fortunately, Dad had insurance to cover just such accidents. The old man tried to back out, but the hood of the Caddy had pushed up and was caught on the rear bumper of Mr. Antonio's car. In his efforts to back out the old man actually pulled the car on the lift a few feet backward. By this time the old hag had come out into the garage and saw me disappear into the storeroom. I slammed the door shut and pressed the lock button on the door knob thinking that would keep out reptilian alien things that had more strength than the average right-tackle for the Green Bay Packers.

Again, it was Dad to the rescue! He pulled into the service station at that exact moment and started blowing his horn to get the attention of the people trying to get me. The old man jumped out of the Caddy and fled around the corner of the station never to be seen again; I guess he decided to give up on ever capturing and eating me. By this time Dad was out of his car and running toward the garage and the storeroom. The old hag hadn't noticed this latest development, as she was more interested in trying to claw her way through the storeroom door! As he came into the garage, Dad picked up a large adjustable wrench that just happened to be laying on the work bench next to the lift, and as he came up behind the old hag he brought it down with all his strength on the top of the old hag's head! Fortunately for me, I only heard the results of this and didn't see what happened. The old hag's head split right down the middle and her darker-than-normal blood splattered everywhere!

Dad yelled in to me to see if I was ok and I told him I was. He told me to stay put and if I came out before he told me to he would give me the whipping of my life. Well, that was fine with me as I could only imagine what had just happened on the other side of the storeroom door. I asked Dad if he was ok and he said yes, but I had better stay put. I didn't mind staying put because hanging on the wall in the storeroom was an oil company calendar with a photograph of a nearly naked gorgeous woman posing above the calendar. I had often snuck into the storeroom to get a good long peek at the photograph.

Dad went to the office and called the police once again while I involved myself with the anatomical study of the human female form on the calendar. *Maybe I will be a doctor after all, especially since I so enjoy studying the human female form. Why, I can already identify breasts, legs, and other interesting parts, which almost makes me an expert already!* My rapt attention to my studying was broken by the sirens of the police cars pulling into the service station. Because my dad had reported a violent attack on both me and the station, the police dispatcher had decided to send three patrol cars with two officers in each. They were only there a few minutes getting the low down from Dad when four of them started combing the area for the old man dad had described to them. Since they never found him, we might assume that the reptilian alien things' space ship beamed him up and sped off a few thousand miles so as not to be seen by any prying telescopes. The other two cops stayed at the station putting up their yellow tape around the "crime scene" and then starting to examine the evidence. I would be stuck in the storeroom for about two more hours before they let me out to question me. The old hag had been bagged by the medical examiner by that time, so all I saw was a lot of blood around the garage near the storeroom. Over the next hour they asked me to tell my story four times, up to the point when my dad arrived and did in the old hag. It was ruled justifiable homicide by the cops and they promised my dad that they would get to the bottom of all this craziness involving me. The strange thing: we never heard any more about it.

Chapter Forty

I would like to tell you that things were even more exciting over the next few days, but absolutely nothing exciting happened for several days. It was off to work with Dad early every morning and home late. It was pump, pump, pump gas and scrub, scrub, scrub the driveway and I washed and waxed a couple of cars during that quiet period. The most exciting thing that happened was that I caught a glimpse of Cookie across the street running around in very skimpy shorts. I knew that I wasn't dreaming, because she was well out of reach and never even looked in my direction. When I was pumping gas I turned so that I would be looking in the direction of Mr. Morgan's restaurant, when I was scrubbing the driveway I scrubbed toward Mr. Morgan's restaurant, when I was sitting in the office twiddling my thumbs I was looking in the direction of Mr. Morgan's restaurant, and even when I was washing cars I constantly glanced over toward Mr. Morgan's restaurant. *Well, at least I have my dreams!*

It was on a Sunday afternoon at the service station that the next interesting thing happened. It had been a very slow afternoon. Dad usually opened around noon to catch the "church crowd," but around 2:15 we heard a loud noise getting closer and closer to our location. We had been sitting around the office all afternoon, except when we were waiting on the two or three customers that had come in, but we got up and went outside to see what was making all the noise. The sound was coming from above and when we looked up we saw a large military-style helicopter passing above the station. We didn't think much about it at first, because every once-in-a-while such helicopters passed over town. We always figured they were either transporting soldiers from one location to another or flying practice missions. However, this particular helicopter made a turn after flying over and headed back toward the station. As we watched it heading back toward us it seemed to slow down as it came right above the station and then it seemed to pick up speed and head off past us to the west. Just as we were about to head back into the office we noticed the sound was increasing again. We looked at each other at the same time and then back up to the sky as the helicopter came back over the station. This time the helicopter stopped in a hover over the station and someone in the helicopter came over a loud speaker, or something like that, and told us to get back into the building and not to come out for the next hour no matter what.

Dad looked at me a little suspiciously, but said to get inside and not to come out until he said I could. I didn't question that and scampered off back to the office. I was watching outside and saw my dad look up at the hovering helicopter and hold his arms up to question what was going on. I looked up at the helicopter and saw a man motioning for Dad to get inside. Dad gave up his little plea for an answer and walked back to the office.

"There's something important going on," Dad said, "if they have cleared the streets like this. They're obviously doing reconnaissance to make sure there's no one outside."

"Why would they do that?" I asked.

"I don't know," he said. "Maybe there's some important politician coming by this way."

"You mean like the President of the United States?" I asked.

"Yeh, like that," Dad answered. "But I doubt if the President of the United States is coming through this little burg. More like one of those important state politicians on a fund-raising tour."

"Yeh, that must be it," I replied.

The helicopter kept cruising back and forth and especially up and down Memorial Boulevard. After about twenty minutes several police cars with their lights flashing started going by and then a large military-looking semi with a flat bed trailer came by with some very large over-sized object under a huge tarp riding on the bed. That was followed by several more police cars with their lights flashing. I couldn't take my eyes off the trailer with something under a huge tarp, because the shape seemed to resemble that of what I imagined a UFO might look like – you know, the "saucer shape." This, of course, made my suspicious and scared little mind start working. *Maybe the police and the military had found the aliens space craft and killed or captured all of them. That would certainly solve all of my problems! God, I wanted to know what was under that tarp.*

Of course, that would never happen because whatever was under that tarp was now government property and would be hidden away somewhere until they found a way to destroy it. And the public would never know that there had been several reptilian alien things prowling around our little town seducing people, especially kids, in a variety of ways so they could kill and eat them. I mean, look at me. I had been seduced by cookies and root beer, a gorgeous blond, and a psychopath who pretended to want to help me after my bicycle accident. And when the reptilian alien things had found out that teenage human males had raging hormones, they used the gorgeous blond identity several times to try and get me. *And it worked every time!* I just couldn't help myself! I was a horny teenage boy after all! It's just a good thing they hadn't used Cookie's identity to try and get me. I would have been like melted butter on a hot biscuit in that case and they would have gobbled me up.

It was at that moment that my daydreaming was broken when Mr. Morgan walked into the office and said, "What the devil do you think that was all about?" he asked my dad.

"You're guess is as good as mine," Dad answered. "Probably some top secret project the government is working on over at MacDill Air Force Base."

"Yeh, that's probably the case," Mr. Morgan said, "but you'd think the press would have gotten wind of it and reported that something was going on."

"Well, when the government wants you know something they'll let the press know," Dad said, "but when they don't want you to know everybody gets silenced. They probably threatened to eliminate people if they said anything."

"Well, my family is pretty scared over there at the restaurant," Mr. Morgan said. "Especially with that danged helicopter hovering over your station earlier."

"We heard the noise and just went out to see what was going on," Dad replied. "Didn't know we were going to cause so much trouble."

"Didn't you get the notice from the police on your door about staying inside today between 2:30 and 3:30?" Mr. Morgan asked Dad.

"There wasn't any notice on my door when we came in around noon," dad answered. "Maybe it blew away."

"It was pretty windy this morning," Mr. Morgan replied.

I had been sitting quietly during this conversation, but had a bright idea as the conversation between dad and Mr. Morgan slowed down. "If Cookie's scared she could come over here and hang out with us," I offered. Both my dad and Mr. Morgan jerked their heads toward me and glared like I was some sort of crazed sex maniac!

"I don't think so, young man," Mr. Morgan said in his best intimidating voice. "You just stay clear of my little girl and we'll get along just fine. Besides, I don't think she's much interested in you."

"Did you get that, James?" Dad asked me.

"Yes sir," I replied. "I didn't mean anything by it."

"I know that," Dad replied, "but Mr. Morgan doesn't want you bothering Cookie."

"Yes sir," I said again.

"I didn't mean to sound so mean, James," Mr. Morgan said apologetically, "but Cookie has too much work to do at the restaurant and at home to have any time for boys."

"Yes sir," I said to Mr. Morgan.

"Well, I need to get back to work," Mr. Morgan said. "Maybe we'll get some customers now that the government is gone."

"That would certainly be nice," Dad replied.

At that, Mr. Morgan turned and exited the office and walked back over to his restaurant. It was after 3:00 and Dad said that we would only stay until five and maybe leave earlier if business didn't pick up soon. I actually hoped that business wouldn't pick up so that we could go home early. Even though there had been a few incidents close to our house I still felt pretty safe there. If what I suspected about what was on the semi's trailer was true, then I might not have to worry about reptilian alien things again. And, on top of that, I wouldn't have to worry about Kelvin any more either. I just wished that Roger's grandmother would let him hang out with me again. I missed my best friend and confidant. *Besides, Roger has the girlie magazine!*

Chapter Forty-one

Then something hit me. "Dad, do you think that man that was with the woman who tried to get me came back and took the notice off the door?" I asked.

Dad gave me that glaring look again and said, "As much as I would like to say no, it's a possibility."

"You won't leave me here alone again, will you?" I asked.

"Don't worry about that, son," Dad answered. "Either your mom or me will always be close by."

"Thanks," I replied.

"You know," Dad said, "why don't we close this joint up and head home? I think we deserve a little break."

"Suits me," I answered.

It only took about fifteen minutes for us to turn everything off and lock up. We got into the car and Dad tried the starter, but nothing happened. After offering up a couple of expletives, dad got out of the car and raised the hood. He checked several things including the battery, but everything seemed fine. By this time I had gotten out of the car and was looking under the hood with him.

"This darned thing worked fine a few hours ago," dad offered. "There weren't any lights on and that battery's almost new. I just don't understand it."

"Could it be the starter?" I asked.

"Nah," he replied. "If it was the starter it would at least be clicking. It isn't doing anything." Then dad noticed something and exclaimed, "Look at that! The plug wires are all missing! Son of a gun!"

"Why would the plug wires all be missing?" I stupidly asked.

"Gee, I don't know," dad replied, "bet it's because somebody took them."

"Then that means that old man must have come back," I said.

"I'm beginning to think you might have something there," dad said. "The next question is how are we going to get home? It's a long walk from here."

"Maybe Mr. Morgan would run us home," I offered thinking maybe Cookie would tag along.

"Well, let's go over there and ask him," dad said.

Mr. Morgan was glad to give us a ride home, but there was no sign of Cookie at the restaurant, so that hope was dashed on the rocks of life as usual. The three of us walked out to Mr. Morgan's car and got in with me in the back. When Mr. Morgan tried to start his car he got the same result as we had. He gave my dad a funny look that dad returned.

"This is a little too strange to be a coincidence," Mr. Morgan offered.

Not wanting to bring up the incident at the station with the old man and the old hag, Dad offered, "You don't think the police or the military snuck around here and disabled our cars do you?"

"You might just have something there," Mr. Morgan replied. "They obviously didn't want us going anywhere while the parade went by."

"Well, let's take a look under your hood and see if the plug wires are missing, too," dad said.

We all piled out of the car and raised the hood to discover that the plug wires were missing in Mr. Morgan's car as well.

"This is one time I wish we had a second car and that your mother could drive," dad said.

"You mean your wife doesn't drive?" Mr. Morgan asked.

"No, she doesn't," dad answered. "Just something she never wanted to do."

"How does she get to work?" Mr. Morgan inquired.

"Rides the city bus," I piped in.

"I'll be danged," Mr. Morgan said. "Don't think we could get along if the little lady didn't drive. Heck, I can hardly wait for Cookie to start driving."

"Yeh, I feel the same way about James," Dad said.

"Let me go back inside and call the wife," Mr. Morgan said. "She stayed home today and she could come and get all of us. I'll just close early, too."

All of us? I thought. *That means Cookie, too. Oh my God!* What would I do if Cookie was in the same car as me? How would I act? Did I look ok? I bet I had grease or something on me somewhere and my hair had to be a mess. *Crap!* I thought. The only chance that I would ever have to be in the same car with Cookie Morgan and I looked like crap and was so nervous I couldn't even stutter! "Oh please, dear God," I prayed to myself, *Please don't let me fart or burp or something when we were all piled into the Morgan's car together.*

About twenty minutes later, Mrs. Morgan pulled into the restaurant. Mr. Morgan and Cookie had been closing up shop while Dad and I sat and waited at one of the picnic-style tables out front. Cookie sat up front between her parents and never even looked at me when she got in the car. Dad and I were in the back. I was too nervous to say anything the whole way home and there was very little conversation among the three adults. Dad offered to repair Mr. Morgan's car for free since they were going out of their way to take us home. It would take a couple of days, however, to get the parts. Mr. Morgan told Dad that was a nice gesture and offered to pick us up the next morning on his way into work. All I could think about was being in the car with Cookie again and her not even recognizing that I was there and me being too nervous to mutter even an unintelligible stutter. I liked to think that I was just shy, but I knew that I was just a big wussie around girls! Heck, I hadn't even kissed Leasure very much after all the time we had been together and, no, it wasn't because there was always someone around. *I was just a BIG wussie! I've got a lot of room to talk about Kelvin being a wussie! Oh well, maybe tomorrow would be different.*

Chapter Forty-two

I slept well that night despite the helicopter, the military parade, the dead cars, and riding home in the same car with Cookie Morgan. However, I did have an interesting dream that I remember with great detail. My dream started with me being on a date with Cookie Morgan. I was sixteen in the dream and had a really hot 1957 Chevy and Cookie was sitting very close to me as I was driving down the road. We were on our way to the Silver Moon Drive-in movie to see the latest release, which for some reason I can't seem to remember – probably because watching the movie was the last thing on my mind. Cookie suggested that we park on the last row because she didn't like being too close to the screen. Well, that was just fine by me and I found the darkest spot still left on the back row. Cookie scooted even closer if that was possible and I slipped my right arm around her shoulder letting my hand droop over her right shoulder and close to second base. The movie started a few minutes later and Cookie sat up and suggested we watch the movie from the back seat. It took us about twenty seconds to scamper onto the back seat and get settled back into our previous positions, except this time Cookie took my left hand and led it straight to second base! Well, it didn't take long for us to become part of the "submarine races" taking place on the back row at the drive-in.

The interesting part of this dream is that I didn't remember the next part of the dream, which had to be the most interesting part. When I woke up from this dream I discovered that I was dreaming that I dreamed it, which meant that I was still asleep and dreaming about dreaming. Only I could dream about dreaming. This will be even more interesting later on, but for now I want to get to the happenings of the next day.

Mr. Morgan picked us up at our house right on time and even dropped us at the front door of the station, but, alas, there was no Cookie riding in with him. I wasn't going to say anything about Cookie, but Mr. Morgan told us that she was coming in to the restaurant later with her mother. She and her mother had an appointment at the doctor's office that morning and had rented a car until theirs was fixed.

After getting the service station opened for business, Dad and I pushed our car into one of the bays so that dad could work on getting the spark plug wires replaced that had mysteriously disappeared the day before. Dad had told me the night before after we got home that he always kept a spare set of plug wires for our car on hand. As a matter-of-fact, dad kept a spare part for everything on our car "just in case." It was a slow morning and after he finished with our car he called the parts store and ordered plug wires for Mr. Morgan's car. He said we'd push his car over to the station when the plug wires came in. Even though the auto parts store didn't deliver, Dad said he'd figure out a way to get them to the station without leaving me alone. As it turned out, Mr. Morgan had his wife go by the auto parts store and pick up the plug wires when they came in. He even paid for them since my dad was doing the labor.

I went over to Mr. Morgan's restaurant and got Dad and me some burgers and fries for lunch and came face to face with the real Cookie when she handed the bag over the counter to me. And, for the first time in the history of my world, she actually spoke to me. Mind you it was just to inform me that her dad said the food was "on the house." I stuttered a "thank you," and managed to walk out the front door without running into it or anything else. At least there was that.

I didn't even have the guts to look back and see if she was watching and waiting for me to stumble and fall flat on my face.

After we finished our burgers and fries I got back to cleaning the driveway and Dad started working on the receipts and bills. A few cars came in for gas and one only wanted his tires checked for proper air pressure. The afternoon was pretty slow until around three o'clock when two and three cars at a time seemed to come in for gas. Dad and I both were working hard to keep up until almost closing time. It wouldn't have been so bad except that part of the "service" we provided our customers was checking the oil, water, tires, and cleaning both the windshield and back window. When the rush was over and it was getting close to time to close up for the day, Dad said that the boom in business that afternoon must have been the result of the little "tie-up" on Sunday when the military stopped traffic and came through with their "hidden treasure." It sounded good to me and I readily agreed.

We were about fifteen minutes from closing time when the Heaven sent vision from across the street came running over to the station to find out if we had heard from the parts store yet. Dad told her we hadn't while I just stood there staring at her. For the second time in my history Cookie looked at me and asked if I had enjoyed the special burgers she had fixed for us.

"Special burgers?" I questioned. "I mean, they were really, really good."

"I put my own special sauce on them," she said. "Just for you."

"Just for me?" I asked. "What's your special sauce?"

Cookie just smiled and winked at me saying, "I'll tell you someday when you're old enough to know." At that she turned and left the station and did just about the sexiest walk back to the restaurant that I had ever seen up to that time, including Monica's.

"What do you think she meant by special sauce?" I asked Dad.

"Beats me," he answered, "but those really were some good burgers. Probably some old family recipe that was handed down to her by her grandmother."

"Do you think my grandmother will hand anything down to me?" I asked dad.

"I rather doubt that will happen, son, since she doesn't have much to hand down," he answered. "The only thing she's got that's worth having is that piece of land her old house sits on in Tennessee, and my brother will probably get that. That old woman still doesn't like the fact that I divorced my first wife and married your mother."

"I've always felt like she didn't care much for Mom and me when we've visited her," I said.

"I'm really sorry for that, son," Dad said. "She could at least treat her own grandson better."

"It's ok," I offered. "I don't think about it much."

I don't know why, but that statement seemed to be all that it took to bring me out of my dream and make me sit up in bed. All I could think about from my dream was that it was weird that I had a dream in my dream. I didn't even think about Cookie, because I found it rather disturbing that I had woken up dreaming about my grandmother. I tried to go back to sleep, but it took about an hour before I finally dozed off. I kept thinking about visiting my grandmother's old place in Tennessee. We had been up there just last year and she still didn't have any electricity running to her house or any indoor plumbing. The outhouse was about twenty yards away from the house down an overgrown path. Of course, that was probably a good thing since it always smelled so bad around the outhouse. My grandmother got her water from a well just outside her backdoor and she cooked on a wood burning stove and heated the house with an old cast-iron Ben Franklin wood burning stove. She used kerosene lamps for light at night, although there wasn't much light that got into the house during the daytime either. Anyway, I thought about all of this and about my primary activity when I was there, which was chasing lightning bugs. Grandmother would reluctantly give me a glass jar with a lid so I could run around the field in front of her house and catch lightning bugs to put in the jar. Of course, I had to let them all go before I came into the house so she could have her jar back. I was hoping that when I did get back to sleep that I wouldn't dream about anything anymore.

Chapter Forty-three

I don't know what kind of pull Mr. Morgan had at the parts store, but Mrs. Morgan dropped the plug wires off the next morning shortly after we had opened up the service station. She said the parts store called just before closing the night before and said the parts were in. Mrs. Morgan had gone by the parts store first thing and brought the plug wires straight to the station. Dad and I walked over to the restaurant and pushed Mr. Morgan's car back across the street and into one of the bays. Dad got right to work on replacing the spark plug wires and was finished with the job shortly thereafter.

Mr. Morgan was very grateful and kept thanking my dad for taking care of his car. Dad told him it was the least he could do for helping us out. Mr. Morgan said that was what neighbors did for each other.

The rest of the day was pretty normal except that I didn't see Cookie over at the restaurant all day, and you can be sure that I was constantly watching for her. I figured that she must have stayed home that day or had something else going on, because a day hadn't gone by when I was at the station that I didn't see Cookie at least once. Dad and I had brought Vienna sausages and saltine crackers for lunch that day so I didn't get to make a trip over to the Morgan's restaurant to see Cookie either. Vienna sausages and saltine crackers were one of my dad's favorite things for lunch. The other was a cold, fried bologna sandwich on white bread spread with butter on both slices. I didn't mind and always just ate whatever he wanted for lunch, but my favorite now was no doubt a burger from the Morgan's restaurant with Cookie's special sauce.

Dad said that Mom had to stay a little later at work that afternoon and that when we closed up we would go downtown and pick her up from work. Since the last couple of days had gone pretty good business wise, he wanted to know if I would like to go out to eat that night at Howard Johnson's Restaurant. Besides, he said, Mom had had a long day and she deserved a night off from cooking. I liked to go to Howard Johnson's because I could order one of my two favorite things for dinner, beef burgundy with egg noodles or stuffed flounder and spinach. Yes, I was one of those nerdy little geeks who loved spinach! I didn't know, or want to believe, when I was fourteen years old that I was a nerd, but that was probably a fact of life. After all, I actually liked school and most of my classes, especially math and art, but not physical education class. My last year of junior high school physical education class was the best, because three or four of the starters for the basketball team were in my class and because I was almost as tall as them they liked to have me on their team in class. The seventh and eighth grades in physical education class, however, were not good. I couldn't somersault over the gym horse, I couldn't climb the rope more than about two feet off the ground, I couldn't do but about three push-ups and four sit-ups, and a couple of times I slipped coming out of the showers and busted my butt on the wet concrete floor in the locker area where everyone could laugh at me.

However, I was a great dancer and a lot of the girls wanted to dance with me and I was a fast runner. In the seventh grade I could keep up with and sometimes outrun the ninth grade athletes around the small lake across the street from our junior high school, but my mom said no when the running coach wanted me to be on the running team. She didn't want me traveling overnight out of town to cities like Tampa, Sarasota, Miami, and Orlando. *Oh well, I wasn't meant to have an athletic career anyway.*

We picked up Mom from her job downtown at the five and dime store and headed straight for Howard Johnson's for dinner. Mom seemed really tired and appreciated going out to dinner. I decided on the beef burgundy that night and dinner went well. On the way home, which was clear across town from the Howard Johnson's Restaurant, I fell sound asleep sitting upright on the backseat of the car – something that I am still capable of even to this day. Well, whether it was the beef burgundy or the fact that things had been quiet the past few days, I started dreaming about a trip to Tennessee to see grandmother.

We were visiting my grandmother and it was around dusk when I had to go to the outhouse and sit awhile. Fortunately, there was still most of the Sears & Roebuck catalogue left and I didn't have to run back to the house to get a new one. There wasn't a light in the outhouse (remember there was no electricity running to my grandmother's house) and it seemed to be getting dark real fast. I was just finishing up when something came in through the three-inch space over the top of the door (modern ventilation, you know). At first I couldn't see what it was, but since it was spewing sparks it only took about two seconds for me to realize it looked like a stick of dynamite! I pulled my pants up as fast as I could and grabbed up what I thought was a stick of dynamite and threw it in the hole! Well, if anything can put out a burning stick of dynamite it's what's at the bottom of that hole! I heard it hit and fizzle out, which also took away what little light it also had momentarily provided.

I hadn't heard anyone or anything sneak up to the outhouse, but that stick of dynamite didn't crawl up over the door all by itself! I was both scared to leave the stinking place where I was almost blown up, but I was also just as scared to stay in the outhouse not knowing what would come over the door next. I decided to get out of there as fast as I could and run back to the house. Dad would get his flashlight and check out the outhouse and the area around it to see if he could find out what had happened. However, when I pushed on the door to leave it wouldn't open. It didn't even budge a fraction of an inch! It was like a big rock or something else that was very heavy was leaning against the door. Then the outhouse seemed to be leaning! Backwards! Someone or something was not only leaning against the door, it was pushing the outhouse over backwards! As it gradually leaned backwards I climbed up on the seat and then on the back wall as the outhouse crashed to the ground. I figured that would make my fall less painful. When the sidewalls and the top of the outhouse fell outward from the impact I sprang forward where the roof used to be and rolled over on my back.

What I saw was unbelievable! Initially I thought I was looking at Mrs. Root Beer Lady, but she was naked! And that was not a very pleasant sight to see, a big bag of skin and wrinkles! Then my eyes moved up to her head to see Monica's sweet smile looking down on me in the moonlight. Moonlight? When I had entered the outhouse a few minutes ago there was only a new moon just starting to form and now there was a HUGE full moon shining down on us. And then she changed into that huge, wide-mouthed reptile-looking thing that had tried to eat me earlier in the summer back in Florida. It started moving toward me with its large white shark-like teeth glistening with saliva in the light of the full moon. I jumped to my feet only to stumble and fall over the smashed sideboards of the outhouse. I was scrambling along on my hands and knees when I felt the reptilian alien thing's claw like hand grab my foot and start pulling me backwards. At that moment I heard a deafening boom that sounded like my dad's gun going off only louder. The pulling at my foot stopped and I fell forward on my face. I turned over quickly just in time to see a headless thing tumble backwards into the weeds.

My dad came running up quickly to see if I was ok and then walked over to where the headless beast had fallen and emptied the other barrel of my grand-mother's double barrel shotgun into the body of what was left of the thing.

"What the devil was that?" Dad asked me.

"I don't have any idea," I lied. "I was just getting ready to come out when it threw a stick of dynamite into the outhouse. I threw it in the hole and it went out. Then the outhouse started leaning over and the next thing I knew it had me by the foot!"

"Whoa, slow down," Dad said. "What do you mean by it?"

"It looked like a giant lizard," I said. "Maybe it was all of the light shining down on us."

"All the light," Dad asked. "There's barely a new moon out and it's very dark."

"I must have been so scared that I thought it was a giant lizard," I offered.

"Well, the last thing I wanted to do tonight is drive into town and tell the police about something happen-ing out here," Dad said.

No telephone at grandmother's house either.

"Why can't it wait until tomorrow morning?" I asked.

"There's no telling what might happen to him if we leave his body out here all night," Dad suggested more than stated. "Some big animal might drag him off and eat him."

"That wouldn't be all bad, would it?" I asked.

"Probably not," Dad said, "but it still wouldn't be right."

At that moment we heard something move in the direction of the corpse and dad quickly turned his flashlight in that direction. The headless man was sit-ting up and at the same time beginning to grow a new lizard head. Dad looked at me with the strangest look on his face that I had ever seen and then reached in his pocket, got two more shells, and shoved them into grandmother's shotgun. He aimed carefully at the thing regenerating itself in the weeds and pulled both triggers at the same time. The blast from the shotgun was deafening, but dad's aim was perfect and the thing was blown into what seemed like a million pieces.

"James, James," Mom said as she was shaking me. "Wake up! What are you dreaming about this time? We're home and if you don't want to spend the night in the car I suggest you get your stumps moving."

"You mean I was dreaming?" I asked as I crawled out of the car. I was now beginning to think that all of my adventures that summer with Monica, the old hag, and the old man were all just dreams. The only thing was that most of the time I didn't wake up from those dreams, because my life seemed to just keep going after those things had happened to me. *It has to have been real! It just has to have been real. Really!*

Chapter Forty-four

I had a hard time getting to sleep that night, because I couldn't quit thinking about my dream of being attacked by one of the reptilian alien things at my grandmother's house. On top of that I couldn't quit wondering about the rest of my adventures with the reptilian alien things that summer. I had read somewhere that real life experiences can often lead to dreams about those experiences and I was guessing that that was what had happened in my case. My encounters with the old hag, the old man, and Monica were all real and their transformations into reptilian alien things was also real and that was why I had dreams like the one I had coming home from Howard Johnson's.

Then I started thinking about my various encounters with Cookie, both in my dreams and in reality. Ok, I knew which ones were dreams, but didn't the other ones have to be real. Like Cookie bringing over the burgers with her special sauce on them? That certainly was no dream and I could prove that tomorrow morning by asking Dad about it. I decided at that moment that I would ask my dad about Cookie bringing over burgers with "special sauce." That would at least affirm that some of what had been going on behind my eyes was real.

On the way in to the service station the next morning I could barely keep my eyes open, because of my lack of sleep the night before. However, I did remember that I was going to ask Dad about the burgers with special sauce. "Dad," I started, "did Cookie bring us some burgers the other day with what she said was her special sauce or was I dreaming that, too?"

"Those were probably the best hamburgers I have ever eaten, son," Dad answered. "If you were dreaming that then you must have drug me into the dream with you."

"Yes!" I exclaimed. "I knew that couldn't have been a dream. Nothing that tasted that good could ever be a dream!"

"I certainly hope not," Dad said. "You've got it real bad for that girl, don't you?"

Beginning to fully wake up and starting to feel like a real man, I explained, "Well, you have to admit that she's a real looker and a guy like me is lucky to have her say boo to him, much less treat him to her special burgers."

"I wouldn't underestimate myself if I were you," Dad told me. "You may be only working in a service station and mowing yards right now, but you'll make something of yourself one of these days. I'm sure of it."

"Thanks for the vote of confidence, Dad," I said and let it drop there for the time being. "What's on our agenda for today?"

"One thing about working in a service station is that it doesn't change much from day to day," Dad offered. "Nothing special today, but I'm hoping to get a couple of oil changes or some other mechanical work. We could certainly use the extra cash these days."

As it turned out that day we not only had an unusual number of people coming in for gas, including a hot college-age babe in a short tennis outfit, but Dad had three oil changes, two tune ups, sold a set of new Atlas tires including balancing and front end alignment, and I had to wash three cars. I guess sometimes when you least expect it your hopes and prayers get answered, especially those that are important. I knew that I could pray twenty-four times a day, once every hour, that Cookie would change her mind about me and have her way with me, but that wasn't really what was important in life at that time. What was important was Mom and Dad making enough money to put a roof over our heads and food on the table and me helping out as much as I could for a fourteen-year-old. I didn't expect my parents to buy me a car when I turned sixteen, I expected to earn the money and buy my own car even if it meant holding down a full-time job when I turned sixteen. And that was exactly what I did my last year of high school. Dad was managing a Star gas station (they only sold gas, oil, and cigarettes) at that time and one of his second-shift men had quit showing up for work. After struggling along and pulling a double shift for two weeks and listening to me begging for the chance to do the job he finally offered it to me.

Now, the second shift usually went from three o'clock in the afternoon until eleven o'clock at night, but since I didn't get out of school until three-fifteen dad let me come in at four and work until midnight. That gave me time to go home and put on my uniform before arriving at work. I had been working at the local movie house downtown after school and some on weekends twenty hours a week for fifty cents an hour. The gas station job paid a dollar and twenty-five cents an hour and I got to work forty-eight hours per week and got time and a half for the extra eight hours! My jump to the big time that school year helped pay for my new car and put gas in it for me to go cruising on my one night off. But, once again, I digress.

The summer was coming to a close faster than I wanted, because for the first time I wasn't anxious to get back to school and see all my buddies. I kept thinking that if the summer could only last a little longer I might actually have a chance with Cookie. When I told one of my buddies this after school started back, he said, "Yeh! Right! And what planet are you from?"

On the flip side of the coin, I also thought that if school were back in session I wouldn't have to worry so much about the reptilian alien things getting me. Surely they wouldn't attack me at school with so many people around, even if they were mostly teenagers. Of course, if there were more than three reptilian alien things and the police and military hadn't killed or captured all of them and since they seemed to like teenagers best, it would be the perfect hunting ground for them.

The next part of my story is the really strange part. Everything at the station seemed to settle down about an hour before our normal closing time and Dad and I were just loafing around the office taking it easy from a very busy, and profitable, day. We had only been taking it easy for about fifteen minutes when a brand new Mercedes Benz 230SL pulled into the station and parked in front of the open bay with the rack. A well-dressed man in a three-piece suit got out of the Mercedes and walked into the office.

"Good afternoon," he started. "The restaurant owner across the street says you're the best dang mechanic in these parts. That true?"

"None better!" I exclaimed quickly.

"Well, I don't know about that," Dad answered, "but I know what I'm doing around cars."

"Great!" said the stranger. "Nobody seems to know what's wrong with my new car."

"What makes you think something's wrong with it?" Dad asked.

"It tends to sputter every once in a while and doesn't have the fast pickup it had when I bought it about six months ago," the man explained to Dad.

"Have you had it serviced since you bought it or taken it back to the dealer to see what's wrong?" Dad asked.

"I don't live close to the dealership, so I took it to a guy near where I live who specializes in foreign cars, but he said he couldn't find anything specific," Mr. Mercedes man told Dad. "He told me that he would have to tear the whole engine down to find the problem and that it would be expensive. Not that the money's the problem, but I don't like being taken to the cleaners!"

"Well, I don't know a lot about foreign cars, but let's have a look under that hood," Dad offered.

All three of us went out to the Mercedes and the man in the three-piece suit opened the hood and raised it up for Dad to have a look. Dad asked him to start the car and he got in and cranked it up. He revved it up when Dad asked him to and turned it off and started it again and revved it again and turned it off again. Dad found the gas line and followed it along until he came to the gas filter. Dad disconnected the line from the filter and removed it. We didn't stock many parts in the station and especially not Mercedes Benz parts, so Dad took the filter over to the parts washer and did the best he could to clean it out. After a few minutes dad walked back to the car and reconnected the gas filter. He told Mr. Mercedes man to take it for a run around the block or down the boulevard to see how it was running. Dad and I went back into the office to wait and see if the man would actually come back. I asked Dad if he thought the gas filter was the problem and he said he thought so, but it would depend on what the guy said if he came back.

About ten minutes later the Mercedes pulled back into the station and up to the front door. Mr. Mercedes man got out and strutted into the office and proclaimed, "You're an absolute genius!" he exclaimed. "That confounded car runs better than when it was new! What did you do and how much do I owe you?"

"The gas filter was especially dirty for some reason," Dad explained. "It almost looked like someone had clogged it up on purpose."

"No doubt someone did," Mr. Mercedes man said. "Now how much do I owe you?"

"Nothing," Dad answered. "All I did was clean the filter. I would look into getting a new one, though, because that one should be in better shape."

"You saved me thousands of dollars and you don't want anything for fixing my car," Mr. Mercedes said. "I am an executive with a large company in the area and you just earned all of our mechanical business, if you want it."

I looked at Dad expecting him to decline the offer, but he said, "That would be a prayer come true. Business has been slow lately and I wasn't sure how we were going to stay afloat. Thank you very much."

"No problem," Mr. Mercedes man said. "We've got four or five trucks needing service now. I'll send them over tomorrow. You get to them as you can. We have plenty of trucks and can miss four or five for a day or so. By the way, the name's Padmier, Trevor Padmier," he said and reached out to shake Dad's hand.

Dad reached out and shook Mr. Padmier's hand and said, "Just call me Slim."

"You got it, Slim," Mr. Padmier said. We'll have the best running fleet of trucks and cars in the state. Goodnight."

"Goodnight," Dad and I both said at the same time and started smiling when we looked at each other.

Chapter Forty-five

I had been taught to pray every day, but not because I wanted things. Instead, I was taught to be thankful for what I had and ask for forgiveness of my sins and only pray for things like good health. Well, I followed this prescription faithfully even when things weren't going my way and now I believed that there were real blessings. This new contract with Mr. Padmier was certainly an answered prayer and Dad was almost giddy when he was telling Mom about it that night. I was not only happy for the extra money this business would bring in, but I was especially happy for Dad and very proud of him for maybe the first time in my life.

Most teenagers I knew at that time loved their parents and obeyed their parents, but most never said anything about being proud of them since most of the kids I hung out with had hard-working blue collar parents. I remember the first time my girlfriend, Leasure, asked me about my dad's career and I beat around the bush trying to think of a fancy name for "gas station jockey." The best I could come up with was that he ran a service station over on Memorial Boulevard. Her response was, "Oh." I should have known at that moment that I wasn't good enough for her, but I was just happy to be able to say that I had a girlfriend. In high school I decided that she had only stuck with me through junior high school because all the other boys were smart enough to know that she was a snob.

Regardless of that I still gave thanks to God that I had a girlfriend. And even though I had never felt proud of my dad before that time, I always gave thanks for my parents and prayed for their health and happiness. I knew my dad was a good mechanic, but I had never bragged about that to my friends. After Mr. Padmier gave Dad all of his company's service business on their cars and trucks, including recommending that his employees bring their business to Dad, I was never ashamed of telling my friends that my dad was the "best darned mechanic in these parts" or, for that matter, anywhere!

I later found out from Mom that the main reason Dad had agreed to take on all that extra work was not to have more money to spend, but to try and start saving some money for me to go to college. I hadn't even given any thought to going to college, because I figured it just wouldn't happen since my parents barely got by. After I got to high school it was always awkward when the kids around me talked about where they hoped to go to college or, in the case of the rich kids, where they were going to go to college. I always answered that I was still thinking about it, because I knew it wouldn't happen. I figured I would just pump gas all my life and barely scrape by like my parents. I did go off to art school when I graduated from high school, but after two years my parents had used up all of the college fund they had saved and I had to drop out and move back home. I did eventually get a college degree, but I had to pay my own way most of the time. For the two years at art school, however, I was very thankful for Mr. Padmier's business.

I was so up because of Dad's success that I couldn't wait for school to start back so that I could brag to my friends about what Dad had done and the resulting business from one of the biggest companies around. However, there was still some time left in the summer and I was still working at the station every day, because Dad was still afraid for me to be alone with all the crazies running around. And, to tell the truth, I was still scared to be alone, too, and what happened the very next day shows why.

Chapter Forty-six

The next morning Dad wanted to know if I was willing to stay home that day and mow our yard since the grass was getting pretty long. He said he thought it would be fine since nothing strange had happened for a while. He reckoned that since the old woman had died that the old man and the younger woman who had tried to pull me into her car had skipped town. I was a little uneasy about staying home alone that day, but I wanted to keep Dad's spirits up and said that I thought it would be fine, too.

Dad left for work first, as usual, and Mom was off on the city bus to work by seven thirty. I hung out in the house until around nine o'clock contemplating my situation for the day. I didn't have to worry about Kelvin as he and his father had moved out of state since his mother had committed suicide. Mr. Kiches had cleanup crews come in and get the house in shape to sell it. I guess word got out about what happened there, because the Kiches house didn't sell for nearly three years. Then there was Roger's grandmother who wouldn't let her little baby come out and play as long as I was around. I had heard through the old grapevine that Roger's mother had blessed out Granny Maleway and told her that I was Roger's best friend and that she should let him hang out with me. However, it didn't do any good and Roger and I were a thing of the past. Next was Mrs. Chyspo, who had lured me back to her house when I had my bike accident and then tried to kill and eat me. However, she did stand up for me against her friend, Mrs. Maleway, when she was trying to belittle me. As far as I was concerned, Mrs. Chyspo's aim could have been better when she clobbered Roger's granny.

When I finally stopped worrying about what was still out there that might cause me harm, I got the mower out of the shed and started mowing our yard. We didn't have a large yard, but it usually took me about an hour to get the whole yard mowed. I always started in the front and finished in the back yard, but today I thought I should get the back yard done first so I would be in the front where people could see me if something happened. I mowed faster than my normal pace, because I wanted to get back inside as soon as possible. Everything had gone smoothly and nothing had happened until I was putting the mower back in the shed.

I had my back to the street picking up the back end of the mower to roll it back into the shed when a voice I had never heard said, "What the devil do you think you're doing in my shed?"

I dropped the back end of the mower and it clanged down on the concrete steps and knocked me backwards on my butt. I scooted around to face the voice, but when I got all the way around there wasn't anyone, or anything. I stood up and peeked around the corner of the shed, but there wasn't anyone there either. I walked slowly to the front of the carport and peeked around the corner to the front of the house and the front yard, but, again, there wasn't anyone there. Then I heard the voice again saying this time, "Get inside before they get you."

"Who are you?" I asked. "Better yet, where are you?"

"That is no concern of yours right now," the voice answered from nowhere and everywhere at the same time. "Now get inside before they get you."

Not being the kind of fool to retreat without answers I asked, "Who's going to get me?"

"The reptilian alien things coming down the street," the mysterious voice answered. "Now get inside!"

Well, seeing the horde of reptilian alien things swarming down the street on their hind legs was enough to get my butt in gear and inside the house. I had just gotten the door locked when I heard what sounded like a giant swarm of mosquitoes hitting the house. I dared to look out through the living room curtains and saw that our house was surrounded by reptilian alien things that were rushing back and forth trying to find an opening to get inside. The strange thing was that they didn't seem smart enough to try the doors, so I figured these must be real reptilian alien things and not the ones that could change into humans. I moved away from the window hoping that none of them had spotted me and settled down in the hallway in the middle of the house. I could now hear them running across the roof as well. I only now thought about calling my dad at work, but the telephone was located next to the kitchen door that went out to the carport and I was afraid that if I was that close to the walls they might be able to sense me.

It was at that moment that the telephone rang, but I was too afraid to answer it. I only hoped that it was my dad trying to call me to see if I had finished with the yard. If I didn't answer the telephone, maybe he would get suspicious and rush home to see what was wrong. The noise outside seemed to be getting louder and louder and I was sure that more reptilian alien things had come to join the first group. There must have been a hundred of the creatures outside trying to find a way inside. This activity seemed like it went on for hours, but it was only about twenty minutes after the telephone stopped ringing that I heard a car pulling into the driveway and screeching to a halt. Just seconds before the car pulled into the driveway the din outside quit instantly. It was almost as if it had never been there.

The kitchen door swung open and my dad rushed inside yelling my name. He saw me cowering in the hallway and ran over to see if I was ok.

"When you didn't answer the telephone I got scared and rushed home," he said. "Why are you huddling here in the hall?"

Well, I certainly couldn't tell him that about a hundred reptilian alien things the size of humans had rushed the house and tried to get in and eat me. So I lied, as usual, about the business of strange creatures that could change into humans and just said that some people came rushing up as I was putting away the mower. I told him that one of them yelled to grab me and I rushed inside and locked the door. I said that they pounded on the door and kept trying the windows and were doing so when the telephone rang. I told Dad that they must have heard the telephone, because they stopped trying to get in after that. However, I wasn't sure so I just stayed in the hall where I could see or hear anyone getting into the house.

"I'm sorry, son," Dad said. "I should have known that whoever is trying to get you would be watching the house and know that you were here alone. What I can't figure out is why they waited until you finished mowing the yard?"

"Beats me," I answered, "but I'm sure glad they did."

"You would've thought someone in this neighborhood would have seen what was going on and called the police," Dad said. "Some neighbors we have."

"I guess most of them are at work and Roger's grandmother won't let him hang out with me anymore," I answered. "If she had seen something she would have just let them get me."

"Well, we all know what she is," Dad said to reassure me that she wasn't liked very much by our neighbors. "Mr. Morgan is watching the station while I'm gone, so you and I better get on back."

"That sounds great to me," I said.

As we were pulling out of the driveway to head back to the service station for the rest of the day Dad said, "Nice job on the lawn, son."

Chapter Forty-seven

I was glad to be heading back to the service station with my dad, but I knew now that the reptilian alien things hadn't all been killed off by the police or the military. It made me wonder what was really under that tarp on the semi-trailer that the government didn't want anybody to see. I still swear that it looked like a saucer shape, which could only be an unidentified flying object, alias UFO. The one thing I couldn't explain was that when my parents showed up everything seemed to get back to normal, if there was such a thing anymore as normal.

Dad and I arrived back at the station and Dad thanked Mr. Morgan for taking the reins while he was gone. Mr. Morgan asked if everything was ok and Dad said yes, that I had locked myself out of the house was all. Just one more thing to make me look like a total idiot to Cookie and Mr. Morgan. Business was slow the rest of the day except for the extra work on Mr. Padmier's fleet of trucks and cars. It didn't take Dad very long to service each vehicle that Mr. Padmier's company brought in, but it was a lot of extra work. The least I could do was "watch the front" while dad worked on the cars and trucks from the company's fleet.

The only interesting thing that happened that afternoon was a Rolls Royce came in about fifteen minutes before closing time and wanted to know if dad could do an oil and filter change before closing. Dad, of course, had to turn down the job since we didn't carry oil filters for a Rolls Royce, but the driver asked if he could bring it by the next afternoon for service. Dad said that he could probably get a filter by then and asked if the there was a special type of oil required for the Rolls. The driver said that any domestic oil was fine, that the owner wasn't that particular, only that the automobile had to be serviced every four thousand miles. Dad usually told his customers that every five thousand miles was fine, but if that was what the owner of the Rolls wanted then so be it. The driver asked if dad could do the job for one hundred dollars including parts and Dad stammered out a definite yes!

"See you tomorrow afternoon then," the driver of the Rolls said. "Is four-thirty ok?"

"That will be fine," Dad said. "We'll hold that time for you."

At that the driver of the Rolls got back in the car and drove off. All of the windows in the Rolls Royce were very dark, so we never did see the owner, if he was in the car at all. Oh well, a hundred bucks for an oil and filter change was probably about eighty-five dollars too much even for a Rolls Royce, but who was complaining? Dad said that was certainly going to be an easy extra couple of bucks to make. I agreed and asked him when he was planning to get the oil filter for the Rolls and he said that he was going to call the auto parts store that afternoon and have it ready to pick up early in the morning, that way I wouldn't be alone at home or the station. I told Dad that sounded like a fine plan.

The next morning we dropped by the auto parts store and picked up the special filter for the Rolls Royce and headed on to the station. On the way down Memorial Boulevard we were sure that we saw the Rolls Royce going by in the other direction, but didn't really think anything about it until we got to the station. The glass in the front door had been completely broken out and the office had been ransacked. The heavy metal desk was turned upside down and all the drawers had been emptied and everything on the shelves had been thrown on the floor and out into the driveway. The Gordon's potato chip rack had been bent double and was wrapped around one of the gas pumps and the oil change rack was turned perpendicular to the way it should have been and hadn't been raised one inch! Everything that was on shelves or racks in the work bays had been thrown on the floor or out front through the closed bay doors. Hanging from the ceiling in the second bay was a hurriedly scribbled sign in what looked like blood that read "Give us the boy or we'll do worse next time!"

"What the devil!" Dad exclaimed more than asked.

"What's that mean, Dad," I asked, as if I didn't know.

"Obviously someone is after you and I'm sorry if I didn't believe you sooner," Dad answered and offered an apology. "Why would they want you?"

"I don't know," I said, "but I'm really starting to worry about both of us. If they'll do all this, what's next?"

"I'm going to call the police right now," Dad said and went into the office to find that the phone cord had been ripped out of the wall and the phone was buried into a dent in one of the other gas pumps. "Well, we're obviously not going to call from here or do any business today so let's go over to Mr. Morgan's and use his telephone to call the police."

"I'm right behind you," I said.

We walked rather quickly over to the Morgan's restaurant to use the telephone. But when we got there we discovered that he hadn't arrived yet. He was usually open by now for the breakfast trade so this was highly unusual for him. We peered in and didn't see anyone inside and then walked around back to see if Mr. Morgan's car was there. His car wasn't there so we decided to wait until he did get in to use the telephone and settled down at one of the picnic tables out front. We sat there for about thirty minutes when Dad decided that Mr. Morgan wasn't coming in that morning for whatever reason.

There were some houses behind the restaurant and we walked back to the first one and knocked on the door. An elderly man answered the door and Dad explained that someone had broken into the station and trashed it and could he use the telephone to call the police. The old gentleman said of course and showed Dad where the telephone was located and Dad called the police to report the break in.

Most of the time the police were very quick to respond to such things, but this time we waited for nearly two hours before they finally showed up and only one police car came with one uniformed officer. "So, what's all the ruckus about?," the cop asked.

"You forget your glasses?" Dad asked in return.

"Don't get smart with me, buddy," the cop replied. "Now what's the matter? Everything looks to be in order to me."

"Maybe you should take your blinders off and look around!" Dad almost shouted.

"Ok, buddy, turn around and put your hands behind your back," the cop instructed dad. "You haven't rested enough."

"Dad, NO!" I shouted. "It's one of them!"

At this the cop reached for his gun, but he reached for it on the wrong side. That was all Dad needed to see to know that this guy wasn't a real cop. Dad reared back and slugged the cop impersonator with all he had and to my surprise the guy went flying backward into the cop car and up onto the hood. Dad was on him in an instant and grabbed him by the collar and slung him head first into the first bay's door. The phony cop's head went right through the small window in the door and his neck rested on the broken glass spurting blood down the front and back of the door.

"Glad he came alone," Dad said.

"You could've handled a dozen of his type!" I exclaimed.

"You're really observant to have seen that he wasn't a real cop," Dad said.

"It wasn't what I saw," I replied. "It was what he said. He said that you hadn't "rested enough," instead of that you were under arrest."

"Still pretty smart if you ask me," Dad said. "I didn't know until he reached to the wrong side for his gun."

"What do we do now?" I asked.

"We obviously aren't going to get anywhere by calling the police again," dad answered. "The officer in this car must have been bushwhacked along the way."

"Yeh," I said, "that must have been what happened." I looked over at the dead cop impersonator and he still hadn't changed back into a reptilian alien thing, so I figured that there must actually be some real people after me. "What are we going to do with the dead phony cop?"

"Not sure," dad answered, "but we need to decide pretty soon."

Chapter Forty-eight

Dad and I decided that the best thing to do was put the dead phony cop back into his car and drive the car somewhere and crash it so that it looked like the phony cop had crashed the car and went through the windshield. We drove the car to a quiet place behind an old abandoned warehouse in a shady part of town.

Dad put the dead phony cop behind the steering wheel and aimed the car toward a solid concrete wall. With the cop car in park, Dad put the dead phony cop's big right foot on the gas pedal revving the engine to a high RPM. Closing the driver's side door, Dad reached in with a piece of pipe he had found nearby and shifted the car into drive. The cop car lunged forward knocking the pipe out of dad's hand and sped headfirst into the concrete wall. The crash was really loud and the dead phony cop did go through the windshield, but to top it off the cop car burst into flames. We got out of there as fast as we could and were back out in front of the warehouse and walking down the street when we heard a huge explosion behind us. Obviously the cop car had exploded and that simply meant that it would be hard for the police to figure anything out about who was in the car or why it had crashed into the wall behind the warehouse.

That night on the local news we heard that a police officer had been hijacked and killed and his patrol car stolen, only to be found later that day burned up behind an old abandoned warehouse. The police figured that whoever had killed the policeman and stole his car had died in the crash. Case closed.

Dad and I had walked about a mile away from the warehouse when dad decided to try and hitchhike back close to the station. A man in an old pickup truck picked us up and dropped us off a few blocks away from the station. When we got back we cleaned up the mess the dead phony cop had left when he crashed through the little window in the bay door. After that we started picking up and trying to put things back in place. Some things had to be thrown away because they had been broken in the wrecking of the station that had happened while we were picking up the filter for the Rolls Royce. *The Rolls Royce! The driver and whoever was in the back of that car did this to the station!* When I mentioned that to Dad he said that he had already figured that one out, but there wasn't anything we could do about it unless we caught them in the act.

No more police came by to see what had happened and that made me believe for sure that the police were part of the great reptilian alien things invasion of our little town. I wondered if this was happening all over the country or whether the reptilian alien things had only picked our town for their feasting on young teenage boys. If this was happening all over the country there should have been something on the news about teenage boys disappearing everywhere, but I had not heard nor seen anything on the news to that effect. And I loved listening to the news because I thought that would make me sound smart if I could talk about what was going on in the world. Adults often seemed impressed that I knew as much as I did about world events. Part of it was paying attention to what was on the television and radio, but part was also that I had a subscription to Weekly Reader magazine that I had first received and read in the seventh grade. Even though it was actually meant for younger kids it was still interesting and helped with my knowledge of the world.

Dad and I didn't talk anymore for a long time about what had happened that day at the service station and then we only surmised what had happened and why. Usually, those discussions were very brief and Dad always managed to change the subject. One thing we surmised, because nothing bad happened for a long time after that, was that the phony cop that Dad had killed must have been the ring leader of the group that had been after me.

It was the first day of school several weeks later when the next incident occurred. Like most kids my age in our neighborhood I rode the school bus to and from school on most days, especially to school. That day, when classes were over, I decided to ride the city bus home from school. I liked riding the city bus, because I could find a seat all to myself and just watch the world zip by outside the bus window without all the screaming and yelling from the other kids. I got on the bus that day and paid my fifteen-cent fair and turned down the isle to find a seat. When I looked up the bus was empty of all passengers except for one attractive blond woman sitting at the very back of the bus. My eyes focused in on her briefly and I realized that it was Monica. My first thought was to get back off the bus and not even stop for a refund, but the bus had starting to move away from the curb and then jerked ahead to a faster speed causing me to fall into a nearby seat. The bus was picking up speed and the driver wasn't bothering to stop for any other passengers. As we sped past one stop I heard the man standing there start cussing and when I looked he was waving his fist at the bus.

I looked back toward where Monica was sitting and she was motioning for me to come back and join her. As usual when I encountered her I was immediately under her spell and got up and started walking toward the rear of the bus, even though I knew better. When I got alongside the seat where she was sitting she reached out and gently took my hand and pulled me toward her. I plopped down on the seat next to her and she leaned over and told me she was glad that we could finally be alone together. Well, let me tell you that this fourteen-year-old young man with raging hormones was getting a little excited, because girls just didn't whisper in my ear anything about being along with them. Besides that, Monica was dressed in her skimpiest outfit to date and you can guess what my eyes were focusing on. Have I ever mentioned that Monica had ample breasts?

Well, when she bent over to whisper in my ear her skimpy and loose little top revealed more real breasts than I had ever imagined getting to see before I was thirty! When her left breast rolled out of the skimpy little top and she took my right hand and placed it on that ample breast I thought I was going to explode in my pants right then and there without ever doing anything!

At that moment the hot skin beneath my hand started feeling cold and scaly and I jerked my hand away from her. I looked down and saw that her skin was turning into the skin I had seen many times on the reptilian alien things and when I looked up into her face her baby blue eyes had already turned black as coal and her skin was changing everywhere. Her tongue started getting longer and began to flick in and out of her mouth and a green slimy substance started dripping from the corner of her mouth. The changing must have slowed her/its reaction time down because I managed to jump up off the seat and started running down the aisle toward the front of the bus. As I got close to the driver he turned and burst out of his uniform as a full-fledged reptilian alien thing and then reached to grab me. I managed to jump back out of his reach, but I heard footsteps coming down the aisle behind me and the swishing back and forth of the tail of the reptilian alien thing that had been Monica. Fortunately for me the driver turning away from the steering wheel caused the bus to swerve off the road and up onto the curb and then crashed into a building. The door popped open and I literally jumped out through it, landing hard on the sidewalk, but I got up and started running as fast as I could not paying any attention to what direction I was heading.

I don't know how long I ran, but eventually I just couldn't run anymore and collapsed on the sidewalk up against the wall of the five and dime where my mom worked. I sat there catching my breath for maybe a minute when I realized where I was. I jumped up, looked around to make sure there weren't any reptilian alien things closing in on me, and then ran through the front door of the store and down the stairs to where my mom worked in the notions department. Mom saw me racing toward her and caught me and wanted to know what was going on. Who was I running from? I explained that the blond woman who had tried to get me at the service station had just tried to get me at school. I told her that I had decided to ride the city bus home, but the only people on the bus were the driver and the blond woman. I told her that I had escaped when the bus driver got distracted and crashed. After that little event it was decided by my parents that I would always ride the school bus in both directions and if I did otherwise and they found out I wouldn't be able to sit down for a week! And you can believe that I rode the school bus from then until I started driving.

Chapter Forty-nine

"James! James! James!" my mom was yelling at me. "Get your lazy butt out of bed! You've been sleeping since six o'clock last night!"

I slowly propped myself up on my elbows and looked around with half-open eyes. "What day is it?" I asked my mom.

"Are you that far gone?" she asked. "It's Sunday morning and it's ten o'clock and your dad is waiting on you to help him with the car this morning."

"What day was it yesterday?" I asked still not quite awake.

"If today is Sunday, then yesterday must have been Saturday," Mom answered, beginning to sound a little annoyed.

"Why would I have slept for sixteen hours?" I asked.

"I guess because you were so tired from your first day of mowing yards," mom replied.

"First day?" I said puzzled.

"Yesterday, Saturday, you took off early to get a head start on mowing yards for the summer and you didn't get home until five thirty," Mom informed me. "You said you were too tired to eat, which was a first and made me think you were sick. You got undressed and went straight to bed around six o'clock. You slept until I just got you up."

"You mean it was all a dream?" I asked.

"What was a dream?" Mom asked back. "Was that why you were doing all that moaning and groaning all night, because you were dreaming?"

"No, it had to be real," I answered. "It was too real to be a dream and besides it was in color." I still sounded groggy and Mom was beginning to look at me suspiciously. "The only thing that was real was you zonking out for sixteen hours," Mom replied. "What did you dream about anyway?"

"You mean the service station didn't get broken into and everything wrecked?" I asked.

"What in God's name are you talking about?" Mom inquired with that same suspicious voice.

"You mean that some really bad people weren't trying to abduct me?" I asked.

"You better hope you've been dreaming or you have a lot of explaining to do young man," Mom said, getting more irritated because I was still propped up in bed on my elbows and hadn't made any effort to get out of bed yet.

"You mean that Cookie didn't make Dad and me some really great burgers with her special sauce?" I asked.

"Cookie? Cookie who?" mom wanted to know.

"Cookie Morgan, across the street from the station at the restaurant," I answered.

Mom reached out and put her hand on my forehead and said, "You're talking like you've got a fever, but your head is cool. The Morgan's moved away over a year ago and they didn't have any children. What else were you dreaming about?"

Still not paying attention to about half of what Mom was saying I asked, "You mean Mrs. Chyspo down the street didn't conk Roger's grandmother on the head?"

"Good Lord, boy, you are as delusional as a crazy bat!" Mom told me matter-of-factly. "Why would Mrs. Chyspo conk Roger's granny on the head?"

"Roger's granny was bad mouthing me to her and Mrs. Chyspo stuck up for me," I answered, but beginning to doubt myself. "And what about Mrs. Kiches next door?" I asked.

"What about Mrs. Kiches next door?" Mom asked back.

"She shot herself while Kelvin and his dad were out and they came home and found her dead," I explained. "There was blood all over the place in their house! I saw it!"

"You weren't having just a dream, son," Mom replied, "You were having a really bad nightmare! That or you've got one heck of an imagination!"

Not thinking I blurted out, "And what about the reptilian alien things that have been trying to get me all summer? Huh? What about them?"

"Your last day of school was Friday," Mom stated. "You know, the day before yesterday, which was Saturday." Mom was really beginning to sound annoyed now. "Summer doesn't start for another month!" Yep, she was really starting to get annoyed.

"You mean Monica wasn't real either?" I asked, without thinking.

"Monica?" Mom asked in a very suspicious voice. "And just who is this Monica?"

It was too late to back out now, so I said, "You know, the hot blond woman that tried to abduct me and that Dad chased off once at the station."

"And this happened sometime during the summer?" mom asked.

"Well, not if I was dreaming," I said in my best sassy voice realizing that as soon as I had said it I was wading in deeper and deeper.

"You get sassy with me one more time, young man and I'm going to wear your skinny little fanny out with the biggest switch I can find," Mom told me in her best "you better believe it" stern voice. And you can rest assured that I believed her!

"How could I have one dream in one night that was about my whole summer experience?" I asked myself more than my mom. "You mean all of what I'm talking about was just a stupid dream?"

"If you don't get your lazy butt out of bed and get outside and help your father with the car you're going to be dreaming about how sore your fanny is and sleeping on your stomach for a week!" Mom said. "NOW GET OUT OF BED!"

At that I literally jumped up and ran to the bathroom to get ready. Even though there had been some really scary moments in what I was now beginning to believe had been a dream, nothing was more scary than my mom yelling at me to get my fanny in gear if I didn't want a spanking. I had learned that the hard way about seven years earlier.

When I came out of the bathroom and wandered into the kitchen, still a little groggy, Mom had already fixed my breakfast and instructed me to sit down and eat. As I was getting settled at the table I asked her if she had heard me talking in my sleep.

She said that around seven o'clock that morning she had come in to wake me up, again, and I was mumbling something, so she let me sleep some more.

"Did you understand anything I was saying?" I asked cautiously not sure if I really wanted to know.

"All I could make out was something about a special sauce and from what I could gather it must have been really special," mom answered. "Didn't get the recipe, did you?" she asked and when I looked at her she was finally smiling.

"No," I answered. "Cookie wouldn't share her grandmother's secret recipe."

At that we both started laughing. I finished my breakfast and then went outside to help my dad work on the car. I just hoped that my sixteen-hour dream wasn't a prelude to what was to come that summer.

"Prelude?" I mumbled to myself standing next to the driver's side front fender and looking under the hood at what Dad was working on. I looked out toward the street when I heard a car coming, just in time to see a big Cadillac going by with an old man driving and an old woman sitting on the passenger side in the front and a knock-dead gorgeous blond woman staring out the back window at me.

~*~

AUTHOR'S NOTE

The Summer of My Fourteenth Year is a story in which the main character is based on me. The part about me mowing yards in a small Florida town to earn money to buy my first car is based on fact. My parents characters are very close to fact (both are now deceased). My dad's service station and me working in it are based on fact. My mom working in the notions department of S.H. Kress is based on fact. Some of the other characters are roughly based on real people that I came in contact with between 1957 and 1967, but the names have been changed to protect the guilty. Guilty only in the fact that they happened to cross my path, or me theirs, during those ten years. However, for the most part the events and characters in this book are purely fiction. I started writing my story in 2007 and it started out as one thing and then early on took a different turn when my imagination started running away from me. Yes, even at 58, I still had an imagination. Stephen King stated in his book, *On Writing*, " . . . good story ideas seem to come quite literally from nowhere, sailing at you right out of the empty sky: two previously unrelated ideas come together and make something new under the sun." I only wish I had read that when it was published in 2000 instead of seven years later. Thank you for taking this journey that I have presented here. I hope that you enjoy reading it as much as I enjoyed writing it.

Jim Meaders

Made in the USA
Charleston, SC
22 June 2010